STEVIE-GIRL AND THE
PHANTOM STUDENT

ANN SWANN

5 PRINCE PUBLISHING
5PrinceBooks.com

STEVIE-GIRL AND THE PHANTOM STUDENT

BOOK TWO

Ann Swann

5 PRINCE PUBLISHING & BOOKS, LLC

PO Box 971

Golden, CO 80402-0971

www.5PrinceBooks.com

Digital ISBN 978-1-63112-206-4

Print ISBN 978-1-63112-207-1

Stevie-girl and the Phantom Student, Ann Swann

Copyright Ann Swann 2018

Published by 5 Prince Publishing

Cover Credit: Viola Estrella

Third Edition 2018

This book is dedicated to all those students who walk the halls like phantoms, hoping their differences truly are invisible.

AUTHOR'S NOTE

Author's note on Tourette syndrome:

A French physician named Georges Gilles de la Tourette first described Tourette syndrome way back in 1885. It is a medical condition that is defined by rapid, repeated, involuntary movements (tics) of the face, arms, legs, and even the body. It begins in childhood and may be categorized as mild or severe. Mild cases may involve nothing more than repeated blinking or throat clearing. Severe cases may include multiple body movements along with vocal tics such as barking or using profane or inappropriate language (this is rare). Boys are 3 to 4 times more likely to be diagnosed with Tourette's than girls, and it is found in all ethnic groups as well as all professions. People with Tourette's have no barriers to personal or professional achievement.

For more information on this disorder, visit The National Tourette Syndrome Association's website: http://www.tsa-usa.org/

Author's note on Albinism:

Albinism is a condition in which a person has inherited genes that do not make the usual amount of a pigment called melanin. It is this pigment that gives color to skin, hair, and eyes. Albinism can affect any race. About one in 17,000 people in America have some form of albinism. It can affect the body in different ways, such as very light skin, hair, and eye color. Those people must take extra precautions to avoid sunburn. Vision is always affected in people with albinism although the degree of impairment varies widely. In fact, the main test for this disorder is a simple eye exam.

For more information on albinism, visit The National Organization for Albinism and Hypopigmentation's website: http://www.albinism.org

PROLOGUE

To us, 1970 was a time of beginnings, but to the country, it was a time of endings. National Guardsmen ended the lives of four students at Kent State College. A hundred thousand marched on Washington to end the war in Vietnam, and in England, Paul McCartney announced the end of The Beatles. It was also the year Jimi Hendrix and Janis Joplin both ended their lives through drug overdoses. It felt as if the whole world was in turmoil.

Our homeroom teacher said not to let the weight of the world stop us from being open to new experiences. In fact she said it was more important than ever that we should be open-minded. I wondered if she'd gone radical on us. For a moment, I thought she might pick up a sign and start chanting.

Come to find out, she was simply prepping us for a new addition to our eighth grade class at Crossroads Junior High. His name was Derol Pavey, and he had something called Tourette Syndrome.

STEVIE-GIRL AND THE PHANTOM STUDENT

1

"What's up?" Jase's voice was low, but then he was never very loud. Guess that's why we got along so well.

I smiled up at him. "Not much." I shifted my books from the crook of one arm to the crook of the other. "What's up with you?"

Jase grimaced. I could tell he wanted to say something.

I elbowed him in the ribs as we made our way across homeroom to our desks in the back corner. "Why are you making that face? What's wrong?"

"Nothing really," he replied, his usually clear green eyes clouded and mysterious. "It's just that, well. Have you heard about Janis Joplin?"

That got my attention. I loved Janis Joplin. Jase had accidentally caught me wailing away to one of her records one afternoon when I was supposed to meet him in front of my house. When I wasn't outside, he had just opened the screen door and came on inside. He said he could hear my yowling as soon as his feet cleared the threshold. After that, I always locked the front door before singing my Janis tunes.

"What about her?" I asked, a pang of unease settling in my stomach like the cherry pit I'd accidentally swallowed when I was about five. Jimi Hendrix, who had electrified Woodstock only thirteen months earlier, had recently overdosed on a combination of drugs and alcohol. And everyone knew Janis was every bit as wild as Jimi. Maybe even wilder.

Jase looked up as several other students entered the classroom. "They found her in a motel room yesterday. She overdosed."

I looked at the psychedelic pink and purple swirls decorating my notebook. Snippets of my favorite Janis song, Piece of My Heart, swirled through my mind in patterns that seemed very similar.

"Oh." My voice was small. I couldn't seem to say anything else. Janis was a big star. She wasn't a friend or an acquaintance, but she was young and famous. She shouldn't have died. She and Hendrix were both only twenty-seven years old. I hated when people just up and died without warning. It happened all the time in my little corner of the world. Even though I had already lost both my Mom and my Gran, I guess I thought famous people should be immune to death or something. Irrational tears started in the corners of my eyes and began a lazy trek toward my chin.

Jase reached across the aisle between our desks. His hand was large and firm when he grasped my shoulder. I'd taken hold of that hand on more than one occasion when he had to help me across a ditch or even the time I had to help him up after he fell down the stairs in the old haunted Taylor mansion. But this show of concern right in front of everyone in the class, this was something altogether different.

I shrugged my shoulder so he would take his hand away.

He didn't get mad or upset. Jase didn't get mad. He understood me pretty well. He knew I didn't like to be the center of attention. I smiled at him to let him know I appreciated the gesture of friendship, but I felt silly sitting there crying over someone who had caused her own demise by doing things that were illegal and stupid.

Somehow, I'd identified with Janis, that's why I'd admired her. She succeeded even though she was different—maybe because she was different. It was as if she had taken her outcast image and made it larger than life. I could never do that, even if I did feel the same way. But I could relate to her, and I could admire her for it, and now she was gone, so I guess now I could grieve for her, too.

I might have sat there wallowing in grief for the whole twenty-minute class period except that Derol Pavey chose that moment to make his entrance.

When he stepped through the door and stood hesitantly in front of the class waiting for Mrs. Flint to acknowledge him, the excitement in the room was as thick as cream, but not nearly as sweet. In fact, there was a sour feeling, as if every student had just run a dozen laps at P.E. and then skipped the showers.

Mrs. Flint took a deep breath. She'd tried to prepare us, but maybe that was part of the problem. We could sense her uncertainty, and it transferred to us as if by electrical current. "Class," she said. "This is Derol Pavey. He is the new student I told you about from the Philippines."

Ahhh, so that explained it. Not only did the kid suffer from something called Tourette Syndrome, he also suffered the dreaded curse of being from somewhere else. His skin was a dusky bronze color, and his night-black hair was shiny and razor-straight.

He peered at us from eyes almost as black as his hair and then the oddest thing happened. His left arm flew up and he barked like a hoarse dog. Rarf. Rarf.

Mrs. Flint grabbed his arm as if to hold it in place, but that only made his other arm fly up. His notebook hit the floor and popped open scattering loose-leaf paper everywhere.

Susan Jansen and Juanita Silva were in their customary front row seats. They immediately jumped up and began to gather the papers. They attempted to stuff them back into the sprung clasps of the blue canvas-covered notebook, but Derol, still barking, suddenly began to pirouette like a stout canine ballerina. Mrs. Flint was dragged around in a circle a time or two before she got wise and let loose of his arm, but it was too late. The class was in tatters, some giggled, others gasped in shock, and some of us simply sat in stunned and silent disbelief.

Then as if summoned by magic, Mr. Terrance, the assistant principal, arrived and took hold of poor Derol and ushered him, still twirling and waving his arms, from the room. We could hear them out in the hall, Derol barking and Mr. Terrance shushing.

Janis was forgotten. Jimi was forgotten. My sadness was forgotten. Mrs. Flint flopped down heavily in her tri-wheeled teacher's chair and mopped at her forehead with a crumpled Kleenex from her sweater pocket.

"That didn't go as planned," she muttered. Then she seemed to remember where she was so she leapt to her feet and clapped her hands together smartly. "Class," she said. "Come to order." She motioned toward Juanita and Sally who were still clutching handfuls of paper. "Girls, bring me all that and let's try and get back on track."

The two girls hurried to the front of the room and turned over their treasure.

"Now," the teacher continued. "I must apologize. I'm certain I could've handled that better. Poor Derol. I'm afraid I made things worse. He really can't help himself. We must all remember that." She patted at her short, fluffy hair. It was obvious to all of us that she had no idea how things had gotten so squirrely so quickly.

"Going to be an interesting year," Jase whispered with a wicked grin.

I couldn't help it. I laughed in spite of myself.

2

Class was finally over. It was only homeroom so we didn't actually have assignments. We just received the weekly announcements and worked on other class work or went to tutoring classes if needed. Mrs. Flint was great. After she got around to taking attendance, she actually sat down and took a deep breath. Then she left class and came back with a steaming mug of what I assumed to be coffee, probably from that no-man's-land called the teacher's lounge. The class was unnaturally quiet out of respect or awe or leftover shock, I'm not sure which. When the bell rang, Mrs. Flint was just sitting at her desk, the daisy-emblazoned mug proclaiming her to be The World's Greatest Teacher clutched in her white-knuckled hand. We all filed by her hesitantly, and I actually had to resist the urge to reach out and pat her as I walked by.

Jase chuckled when we were safely in the hallway. "The rest of the day is bound to be a little anti-climactic."

That was Jase, always using writer-speak. He was a pretty good writer actually, so I guess it wasn't surprising that he spoke that way, too.

"Bound to be," I agreed. "But what about that poor boy, Derol? How horrible that must be for him."

Jase nodded, deep in thought. "Sad." He shoved his blond hair off his forehead roughly. "Wonder how he can stand it?"

I knew he didn't expect me to answer. He was just thinking out loud. We stopped in front of my next class, pre-algebra. "Hey." His voice was serious. "You okay?"

I smiled. "I'm okay. I just feel kind of weird." I started through the classroom door. Mr. Waltzen, the math teacher, did not brook latecomers. He would stand like a statue interrupted in formation, chalk in one hand, pointer in the other, and stare at anyone who came in late. It was enough to make the hair on the back of my neck stand up. I had never had the stare directed at me yet, and I didn't intend to start a new trend today. But Jase reached out and grasped my elbow.

"See you at lunch." His green eyes were mild but deep. He had a pretty good stare himself.

I laughed self-consciously. "Okay. See ya." I scurried into the class like a little mouse caught in the sudden kitchen light.

It was hard to concentrate. Everyone kept glancing at the door half-expecting it to fly open and admit Derol the Whirling Dervish. Some kids were already calling him The Dervish, and I heard Sandy-the-quarterback refer to him as the Tasmanian Devil. But Derol didn't come in and I was more than a little relieved. I couldn't imagine what Mr. Waltzen would do with Derol.

When the bell rang to end class, I swear I heard a collective exhale as we all rose from our seats and filed out. Laura Gonzales walked along beside me. She was quiet, like me, but she was a good student and friendly if you talked to her first. I think she was shy.

"I heard what happened in Mrs. Flint's homeroom this morning," she said simply. "Aren't you in her class?"

I nodded. "It was something. What did you hear, exactly?" I shifted my books to the other arm and waited.

Laura ducked her head as if I'd accused her of gossiping. I hadn't meant to sound harsh, I was just curious as to what was being said. Rumors have such a way of multiplying even in the space of an hour. "The boys who sit behind me were saying that new guy was crazy or something. That he was flinging Mrs. Flint all over the classroom."

Giggles bubbled up out of me before I could stop them. That was a pretty accurate description of Mrs. Flint, but I certainly didn't like the first part. "Sandy, huh?" I glanced at Laura and she looked away. That confirmed what I suspected. He considered himself an expert on anything and everything that happened at the eighth grade level. He'd been that way ever since he'd made the All Star team in Little League way back in fifth grade.

"Don't worry," I said nonchalantly. "Derol isn't crazy, and he wasn't trying to hurt Mrs. Flint." I don't know why I was defending him so vigorously. I didn't even know him. I suppose it was that same old outsider thing that made me admire Janis Joplin. Or maybe it was the underdog thing. I know I often felt like both an outsider and an underdog. I think it had to do with the fact that I had neither a mother nor a father.

Gramps did what he could. He had taken me to Brownies and Girl Scouts. We baked cookies together, and he taught me how to ride my bike. He wasn't much at makeup and hairstyle advice—and Amber Haynes always made sure I was aware of that—but I'd been braiding my own hair since I was old enough to pull a comb through it so that's how I wore it, in one long fat braid or two long skinny ones. I hadn't got up the nerve to ask Gramps if I could wear makeup yet. I wasn't even sure if I wanted to.

The rest of the morning went by without incident. We were studying integers and negative numbers in math...so far, so good. Jase hated math, but I didn't mind it so much. It was challenging. We both liked to read—that was another thing we had in common. Jase also liked to write. His second elective was creative writing. He wrote short stories and poetry, and he swore if I told anyone about the poetry he'd hang me up in a tree by my pigtails. I hated when he called my braids pigtails. I should probably stop wearing them altogether. It was a change that I didn't want to make. Most kids my age were in a hurry to grow up. I couldn't really understand the rush.

FINALLY, lunch. Jase and I always sat at the outdoor tables with Billy Bob. We could sit outside right up to the Christmas break. West Texas didn't get icy cold until January, and when it did get really cold, we'd grab a table inside. But outdoors was always better as far as we were concerned.

Today might be different, though. Just as we sat down at our usual table, we heard Sandy's voice on the other side of the patio. He was retelling everything about Derol's brief appearance in school this morning. "I was in Mrs. Flint's class when he came in," he was saying. "Man, that kid was twirling like the Tasmanian Devil."

Laughter erupted at his table and the tables near him.

"Why does he do that?" I muttered.

Jase and Billy both shook their heads and looked away. The entire patio grew quiet. I glanced up to see Derol Pavey standing uncertainly in the doorway, a sandwich tray in his hands.

The air was still—not even the resident grackles dared break the silence. Finally, someone cleared his throat, and Derol walked shakily to an unoccupied table near ours. Those of us from Mrs. Flint's homeroom were all on the edge of our seats, waiting for him to erupt and throw his tray or start barking like this morning. But he sat quietly, unwrapping his sandwich as if it were his only Christmas gift and he didn't want to tear the paper.

He must have sensed me staring, for suddenly he glanced up and caught my eye. I smiled tentatively. He ducked his head and took a huge bite of ham and cheese.

That's when the giggling began again.

I looked toward Sandy's table. He was gone. This time it was coming from one of the girl's tables. Probably not laughing at Derol. Probably just a coincidence, someone told a joke or something. I turned back to my own bologna and cheese sandwich, but abrupt movements made me glance toward Derol's table.

His leg was jiggling madly and it seemed as if the bite of sandwich he'd taken was stuck in his throat.

Jase and Billy Bob were as still as death beside me. The girls' slinky laugher rode the brilliant fall breeze and settled over us like chain mail, bright and cold. I was pretty sure Missy Bridges was in that group. She was Amber Haynes's best friend. And she had a very public crush on Sandy Morrison. It was almost as apparent as the crush Joanie Lamp had on Jase for the last couple of years. I can honestly say I hadn't shed any tears when her dad was transferred to Austin.

"Hey," I said jovially, "anyone see The Mod Squad on TV last night?"

Jase looked down at me as if I'd sprouted a horn, but he didn't have a chance to answer because Derol suddenly jumped up and dashed across the patio. He uttered a single Rarf! as he fled. Apparently, he'd controlled himself as long as possible.

My sandwich turned to sawdust in my mouth. I couldn't take another bite. Beside me, Jase was wrapping up his own lunch stuff. He had already eaten most of his though. Billy Bob was still plowing through his food as if nothing had happened. Billy was that kind of kid. He didn't really notice what was going on around him unless it fell down and conked him on the head. That was usually a good thing. It kept him out of a lot of trouble.

Jase handed me a carton of chocolate milk. He always bought two. "Here," he said. "You need this more than I do."

I didn't argue. He was right. If I couldn't eat, at least I should try to drink something. I just felt so bad for the new kid. He couldn't help how he was, but how could he possibly cope with his Tourette Syndrome and all the idiots making fun of him, too?

We threw our trash away and headed back to class. Jase and I were off to our second electives, choir for me and creative writing for him. Billy was off to his consumer math class. Billy only got one elective—football—and that took up so much time he wasn't allowed another. But he didn't care. He said it just saved all his energy for the game. Football was his life when he wasn't with us.

After our electives, Jase and I met back up for language arts, the class we usually just called English. This year we were concentrating on literature and whole language grammar. That means we didn't have grammar books anymore. The teacher just used whatever we were reading and made our grammar lessons go along with it.

As a class, we were reading The Outsiders by S.E. Hinton. Jase had been very intrigued to learn that the author was only a teenager when she had written the novel. When he found out she was in college now, I thought he was going to leap up and run out the door right then in search of her.

As usual, we'd both read the book within a few days of it being assigned. In class, Mrs. Kennedy would assign a chapter or two every few days, but who can read a book that way? Together, Jase and I were already trying to think of ways to make our book report stand out. We were lucky Mrs. Kennedy let us choose our own partners for the assignment. We were thinking of doing parallel timelines showing how the two different social groups, the Greasers and the Socs, co-existed in the same town but in almost different universes.

Jase thought we should actually rewrite important scenes from the novel as science fiction. I was withholding my judgment on that one. After all, he was the writer, not me. He said I would be the idea man. I wasn't sure how I felt about that either.

By the time class was over, I was more than a little ready to head to the band hall and blow off some steam. We walked over together for our last period of the day. Jase immediately headed for the percussion section where he picked up a snare and began to bang out a steady rhythm. Guess I wasn't the only one who needed to let off some steam.

Mr. Brown, the band director, came in and called us all to order and we started right in on scales. I loved band. For fifty solid minutes we thought of nothing but notes and rhythms. We were getting ready for the Thursday night junior high football game where we would try out our John Philip Sousa marches and our Henry Mancini song, The Shot in the Dark, better known as The Pink Panther song. The music we practiced in class was the same stuff we would practice out on the football field as we worked on our formations.

As soon as were finished, Billy Bob and the team would take the field. They practiced every afternoon. Small town Texas thrived on football, and all its trappings.

3

Maybe all the talk about science fiction and parallel universes is what caused me to have such vivid, unsettling dreams that night. It was as if a person was visiting me from another planet or something. The person, I couldn't tell if it was male or female, looked like a kid, but it was hard to tell the way it was standing in front of me swishing back and forth like a whisk broom in the hand of a mad man. And the entire dream was in black and white. The swishy person was all in shades of black with long, strange white hair. I couldn't tell if the black clothing was a long dress or a longish black coat. The figure was standing beneath the cool curve of a high, brick archway.

It was eerie to say the least. But I didn't tell anyone about it. I didn't know how. It was so weird, so unlike anything I'd ever dreamed before. I sort of hoped it would just melt away like cotton candy on my tongue.

Of course the entire time I was getting ready for school, wisps of the dream came floating back to me. Brushing my teeth in front of the bathroom mirror, the white toothpaste foam reminded me of the person's frothy white hair. Even the back and forth motion of the brush across my teeth recalled the way the figure moved. What could it be?

I stared into the mirror for so long, thinking and remembering that I began to wonder just who it was that was staring back at me. My brown eyes looked deeper than they should have, and the small bathroom behind my shoulders seemed much too large, the few morning shadows darker than they were a moment before.

I slowly lowered my toothbrush and examined my own familiar face. Why did it feel like I was looking at someone else? All the planes and angles were the same, the tanned skin wasn't changed, and the streaky brown hair was just as it always was this early in the morning. I rinsed my toothbrush and placed it in the holder without taking my eyes from the mirror. Then I picked up my hairbrush.

It was beginning to really freak me out, this feeling that the person in the mirror was someone else standing in another bathroom that was almost, but not quite, the exact opposite of mine. I closed my eyes and began to pull the brush through my hair.

When I opened my eyes, I almost screamed. The reflection in the mirror was looking away from me. It was looking toward the door.

My flesh tried to crawl off my bones.

The face in the mirror, the one that should have been mine but somehow wasn't, slowly turned back toward me. Then it began to change. First, the hair fluffed and brightened, then the eyes grew lighter as the skin began to pale...that's when the figure began to shake and shudder and twitch back and forth like the end of an old movie reel left flapping when the lights come back on.

I still had the hairbrush half-buried in my thick hair. Suddenly, I yanked it through and dashed from the room like a track star approaching the finish line.

I started to yell for Gramps, but instead I divided my hair into three parts and braided it quickly. I'm not a baby, I don't need Gramps to tell me I scared myself silly thinking about a nightmare. I secured the fat braid with an elastic band, then grabbed up last night's homework to stuff it into my notebook. I hazarded one last glance toward the open bathroom door—what if that me-not-me person is standing in there, waiting? I slipped my jacket off the hook on the back of the door and stood silently, listening. Was that a small sound? Was it in there, swishing back and forth, trying to escape from the mirror?

I lost my nerve and hurried to the kitchen for breakfast.

Gramps was drinking coffee and reading the newspaper. "Morning," I said, heading for the fridge, hoping the tremble in my voice was only apparent in my own head.

"Mornin' Stevie-girl," he replied, nose still buried in newsprint. "You sleep okay?"

"Mmph," I mumbled, pouring juice and taking a big gulp quickly. "How about you?" I grabbed a couple slices of bread, dropped them into the ancient toaster, and got out the butter and jelly. Gramps had fried bacon, and I nibbled a strip while I waited. The coffee smelled heavenly, but Gramps only let me indulge on weekends, occasionally. Certainly never on school days, but man, today I could have used some.

Instead, I poured cold milk into my favorite jelly glass—it had pictures of Fred Flintstone and Barney Rubble on it—then added a couple teaspoons of Nestle's Quik chocolate powder. It took a while to stir it, but the wait was worth it.

My toast popped up and I pinched it from the toaster gingerly, plopping it onto my plate along with a pat of butter and a blob of grape jelly. With a butter knife—what my mom used to call a case knife—I smeared the butter and jelly onto each slice, making certain to coat the bread all the way to the edges. Then I took my glass of milk and my plate and sat across from Gramps at the old Formica table.

Gramps slid the last two slices of bacon toward me and I laid them on one slice of toast and covered it up with the other so that I had a bacon and jelly sandwich.

"Looks good," he said.

I chewed and swallowed. "Be better if it was one of Gran's hot biscuits, but it'll do."

"Guess you're just gonna have to break down and make us a batch." Gramps smiled.

I nodded. "Guess I will." I gulped half the milk in one long drink. Jase would've been proud. "First, I've got to teach Mr. Pearcy how to bake a chocolate cake." Mr. Pearcy was an old friend of the family whose wife had died last year. He hired me to help him cook, take care of the house, and learn how to do the laundry—though, truthfully, he had that under control. It was just the cooking and cleaning I was really helping him with now.

"Maybe you can bring your old Gramps a slice, too." He stood up and began to clean off his side of the table. "Chocolate cake sounds pretty complicated. You might have to make a couple of them before he gets the hang of it."

I laughed. "I'll bring you some, too, Gramps. But you know what?"

"What's that, sugar?"

"I think Mr. Pearcy likes to bake. He could easily buy a ready-made mix and just follow the directions, but he says he would rather measure all the ingredients and sift them together just like his wife used to do." I thought back to the last time I'd been over there, a couple days earlier. "You should have seen him in Mrs. Pearcy's apron—"

Just then, Jase appeared at the back door. We had started riding our bikes to school together at the end of last year after all that business with the haunted house. We hadn't been back there anymore. I sort of wanted to, though. It's like my Gramps said, that old house is almost like a magnet.

"C'mon in, Jase," my Gramps said. "You had breakfast?"

Jase nodded and flicked his hair off his forehead. "Yes, sir, thanks. I had cereal at home." We went through this routine almost every day. Gramps always offered, and Jase always declined. He had some sort of streak inside him that seldom let him accept things from other people. Don't want to be a burden, he'd told me once.

"You kids have a good day at school," Gramps said as he picked up his lunch box and pulled on his jacket. He was the daytime dispatcher at the Crossroads Police Department. He had to take lunch because he didn't get a regular lunch hour, just ate at his desk among the radios and telephones. He stooped over and touched his lips to the top of my head. "Love you, girl."

"You too, Gramps," I replied. "Have fun at work."

Before my Gran died, Gramps had been a regular police officer. But since it was just the two of us now, he had changed over to dispatch so that he didn't have to pull the overnight shifts like the regular officers do. Even though I think he missed the excitement, I was really glad he changed. Staying overnight with a babysitter would have been embarrassing. I was plenty old enough to stay home alone in the daytime, but Gramps said overnight was different. If Karla hadn't moved off to California with her mom and grandparents, I could've stayed with her. That would've been an adventure.

So Gramps sacrificed his job and took one that paid a lot less and chained him to a desk all day. When I tried to tell him how much I appreciated all he had done for me, he just waved his hand at me and said, "Pshaw! Ain't nothing I wouldn't do for you, Stevie-girl. We're family."

That's something Jase didn't really have anymore, not since his brother Rusty had joined the Army and his folks had become obsessed with worrying about him. Not that there's anything wrong with worrying about one kid, but it seemed like they'd forgotten about their other kid. Poor Jase. Sometimes I wondered if that was why he hung around with me so much. I didn't have the typical family, but I certainly had a good one.

I gulped the rest of my milk, ate the last bite of sandwich, and ran water in the sink so that the dishes could soak. Normally, I would go back and brush my teeth. This morning, I'd brushed them before breakfast because the weird dream had slowed my thinking and disrupted my routine.

There was no way I was going back in the bathroom anyway. Not right now. But you will be coming home alone after school. Wouldn't you rather know if it's still in there, now, before you leave? That was my common sense talking to me. It always tried to make me do the sensible thing. Sometimes I listened to it, sometimes I ignored it.

Should I get Jase to go in there with me? Could I do it without telling him why? I intended to tell him about the dream, but I didn't know if I was ready to share the mirror thing yet.

"You ready?" he asked, startling me out of my reverie.

I rinsed the handful of dishes and set them in the drain board to drip dry. "Almost," I said. "I—I just want to brush my teeth right quick." It wouldn't hurt to brush them again. Give me an excuse to look at the mirror once more, just so I'd know.

Jase didn't argue. It was another part of the morning routine. I was just moving a bit slowly. I guess he picked up on it. "Okay." He spread out the newspaper and began to read.

How was I going to get him to go in the bathroom and check out the mirror if I didn't admit what I'd seen?

"Um, Jase?" I stood uncertainly in the kitchen doorway. We had a few minutes before we needed to be on the way.

He looked up. "Yeah?"

I fidgeted with my braid and shifted from one foot to the other. Usually, it took a lot to frighten me, but when I'd seen myself in my own mirror looking away toward the door instead of right back at me, well, that had really freaked me out. "Could you..." a sudden stroke of brilliance hit me. "Could you come into the bathroom and see if you can get my ring out of the drain?"

The look on his face was the definition of perplexed. "I've never seen you wear a ring," he said.

Trust him to notice something like that.

"I know, it's—it was my Mom's." I hated lying to him. I crossed my fingers behind my back. It wasn't a bad lie. It wasn't a lie of profit, as my Gramps would say. I wasn't lying to gain anything or hurt anyone. It was just a little white lie...man, I went through this every time. I hate lying of any kind, "Just come look, would ya?"

I turned around and hurried toward the bathroom, hoping he would follow.

But I didn't go into the bathroom. I stood off to the side, just inside my bedroom door. The bathroom was in the hallway between my room and Gramps's room. It wasn't a very big house.

"Did you drop it in the sink?" he asked, ducking a bit to go through the bathroom door. When had he gotten so tall? Over the summer? Wait, I was with him all summer. Wow. Guess you just don't notice things when you're right there at the time."Yeah," I said, fingers still crossed behind my back.

I took a breath and glanced inside. Jase was bent over, gazing into the drain. I looked at the mirror above his head, but there was nothing to see except the reflection of the white tile wall behind him.

"Got a flashlight?" he asked. "I don't see it, but a light would help. Might have to take the p-trap off."

I could tell he was talking more to himself than to me. "Oh," I said. "Look! Here it is. I didn't drop it in there at all." I picked up my Mom's old wedding ring out of the jewelry box on my dresser. I did have her ring. At least that part hadn't been a lie.

Jase raised his head slowly. "What's up, Stevie?" He gazed at me suspiciously. "You're not a very good fibber."

I slumped to my dresser chair. "Just let me brush my teeth, then I'll tell you."

He nodded and walked back to the kitchen.

Running water on my toothbrush again, although it was still damp from a half hour ago, I added a dot of paste and quickly brushed the jelly off my teeth. That was just another of my have-to habits. I hated to leave the house with dirty teeth. I spat, rinsed, and raised my head to blot my chin with the towel. My reflection was staring at me like always. But something was wrong.

"Jase?" I called out quietly, not wanting to alert the girl in the mirror (as though she couldn't see my mouth moving—even though hers didn't).

Jase came quietly back down the hall.

The person in the mirror, the me-not-me, began to fade like mist on a sunny day. First the edges began to blur, then the features, then the entire shape began to shimmy. "Hurry," I called.

He stuck his head into the small room and looked at the mirror. I was still staring at it, but now it was just me again.

I tried to explain what I'd seen. "It was a girl," I said. "She looked like me, only not just like me. In my dream I think it was the same person. At first I couldn't tell if it was a boy or girl, now I'm sure it's a girl."

Jase was watching my face in the mirror. "C'mon," he said,

taking my elbow. "We're going to be late if we don't leave right now. Tell me on the way."

I nodded. I realized I'd been rambling. Jase would believe me when I was able to explain it. That's how we'd first become friends, when he'd recruited me to help him solve the mystery of the phantom pilot that had been haunting him.

He stepped aside and let me go into the hallway first. I couldn't help myself. I glanced back just in time to see the flickering image of the me-not-me girl in the mirror. She was twisting like a runaway kite in a whirlwind.

I gasped, and Jase spun around. "What was it? What did you see?"

"Is she gone?" I had both hands over my eyes.

Jase looked again. "No one's there."

"In the mirror?" I still couldn't bear to look.

He pulled my hands away from my face. "It's all clear," he said, still holding onto my hands. "C'mon, we have to go."

"Okay." I tried to pull my hands away. Jase grinned and held onto one of them. I sighed loudly. "Now I know how you felt when the phantom pilot was appearing in your bedroom every night. If that girl ever appears in my closet like Mr. Gilpin did with you, I think I might lose my marbles."

Jase just tugged me along behind him, picked up my books and the jacket I'd slung over the back of the kitchen chair, before heading to the door. Jase really hated to be late. One more thing we had in common.

4

We rode swiftly at first. When we came in sight of the old elementary school, Jase slowed and almost came to a stop. "Heard they're thinking of tearing it down," he said.

I couldn't speak. A chill wind had blown up and the rustling leaves and brisk air were enough to render me speechless. Something about the old building felt wrong today. I'd passed it hundreds of times in my life. We rode by it every day going to school. It was a dark brown brick building with arched windows that were grimy with years of West Texas dust. Compared to the new elementary four blocks away, this one wasn't very large. But it was elegant, somehow. The curved windows and brick courtyard gave it an air of gentility that the modern glass and concrete school just didn't possess. My mom had gone to school here. It had closed down shortly after the newer school was built, over a decade ago.

"You okay?" Jase had started riding again, slowly.

I nodded. I still couldn't seem to speak. As we put the school behind us, I turned for one more look and there in the window beside the front door, a small face was looking out. She had wild white hair and pale, pale skin.

"Look!" I cried.

Jase spun his bike around. It was too late. The image had already faded back to black.

"Same girl?" he asked.

"I think so." My voice was weak. I hated when that happened. "Man, I'm not digging this, Jase. Not at all."

He laughed and nudged my front tire with his front tire. "It'll be okay. I'm here to help, remember? Just like you helped me."

I tried to feel reassured, but it was just so creepy. "If you say so."

"We'll do some investigating after school," he said. "We'll figure it out. I promise."

We locked our bikes in the rack near the side doors and hurried in to homeroom. Plastered all over the hallway were handmade posters advertising the upcoming Halloween Dance being put on by the seventh- and eighth-grade classes. Every year the classes held a costume contest along with the dance.

Derol Pavey was already in his seat when we arrived. He was in the last row near the windows, the first desk on the row. I think it was the only one available. I'm sure he would have preferred to be at the back of the room.

Jase and I made it to our seats just before the bell rang. Mrs. Flint came in with her mug of coffee and placed it on the desk. If she realized Derol was there today, she didn't say anything. She started off as always by calling the roll. Everyone was present and accounted for. In our small school, everyone tried to have perfect attendance because at the end of the year the class with the highest percentage of perfect attendance was treated to an all day picnic at the Sandhills State Park. Our homeroom was determined to win it. We seemed to have an abundance of competitive students in our room. Maybe it was because we had an abundance of athletes in our room.

"What do you think about the dance?" Jase asked, as we were waiting on Mrs. Flint to finish calling the roll.

"I don't know, why?" I was too distracted with my mirror person and Derol Pavey to think of anything else.

Derol was sitting ramrod straight, his shiny black hair gleaming under the fluorescents. I liked how it appeared to be longer on one side than on the other, and I wondered if that's the way they wore it in the Philippines.

"Just start thinking about it," Jase said nonchalantly.

I looked at him. Start thinking about the Philippines? He wasn't even looking at me, how could he possibly know, or guess, what I was thinking?

He was studying something in his notebook.

"Think about what?" I finally asked.

Still not looking at me he said, "The dance."

"Why?" Then it occurred to me. He wanted to know if I was on the decorating committee, or on the judges-selection committee. The student council had voted to have contests not only for the best costumes, but also for the best limbo dancers, and maybe even for the best twisters if Mr. Terrance would hurry and grant his approval.

"I'm on decorating," I said. "Aren't you?" Most of the band members were going to decorate. I'm not sure why, it just worked out that way.

"Not that," he said in a low voice. "I meant, you and me. What are we going as?"

Well, now I was really flummoxed. "Oh!" I said when the light bulb exploded in my brain. "You mean what costumes?"

"Right." He didn't look up.

I opened my mouth to speak. My heart started to jump as if I had already danced a jig, but I had to make sure I understood him correctly. I was going to say, "We're going as a couple?" However, I didn't have the chance because that's when Mrs. Flint got to Derol's name on the roll.

"Derol Pavey?" she asked a second time.

I wanted to say he's right there, everyone can see that he's right there, but of course, I wouldn't say that. It would be rude. Besides, I didn't want to start off the day with a trip to the principal's office.

Derol raised his head. He was trying to get out the word "here." Everyone near him could hear the clicking in his throat, but "here" just wouldn't come out. Instead he yelled, "Help!" Everyone began to snicker.

That made me so angry. Couldn't they see that he was trying to fit in? I had to do something. That word, help, got to me.

Without thinking, I leapt to my feet, overturning my desk in the process. I hadn't intended for my desk to crash over like that, I was just going to jump up and pretend I had to rush to the restroom or something—like that wouldn't have been embarrassing. Flipping the desk worked even better. The whole class looked at me instead of at Derol.

Jase jumped up and righted my overturned desk. Mrs. Flint gazed in my direction as if she'd never seen me before.

"Sorry," I said. "Sorry, sorry, sorry. I just—" I wasn't sure what was about to come out of my mouth. It didn't matter. Suddenly, Derol found his voice.

"Here!" he sang out, loud and clear. And then, wonder of wonders, he smiled right at me.

I smiled back. Then I sat back down at my desk while Mrs. Flint proceeded to call the rest of the roll. The remainder of the class period passed quietly. It seemed as if everyone was simply waiting for the next round. The dance was forgotten. Jase and I took out our homework and compared notes on The Outsiders. We were having a test over the first few chapters today.

When the bell rang, we got up and began to file out quietly. Derol stayed in his desk. I think he was simply avoiding the crowd.

By lunchtime, the homeroom hijinks were all over school, again. Except this time, people were saying I had fallen out of my desk. Oh well, I didn't care. I was having a bit of trouble convincing myself I had actually done it on purpose, too. As much as I hated being the center of attention, I guess I hated for people to be made fun of even more. My Gramps always said I had an altruistic streak as wide as the Mississippi River. I had to look that word up to find out that it just meant I was always for the underdog. He said I inherited that from my mom who probably inherited it from my Gran.

He also said that if my mom hadn't been so certain she could help my dad, Steve, she might still be around today. "She always saw the best in everyone, no matter how many times they let her down," Gramps had said with a sigh. Then he'd hugged me and told me not to let the altruistic streak override my common sense. "Always put Stevie first, keep her safe. Then you can help the other person." This was a little talk we'd had after Mr. Pearcy had relayed our visit to the haunted house to my Gramps over coffee at the diner one morning. Gramps had mulled it over for days before we had one of our chats on the back porch, him in his rocker, and me in the swing. "Remember," he'd said seriously. "You're all I've got left. You've always got to think of us before anyone else."

I decided he meant I had to stay out of trouble and use my common sense to avoid getting into another situation that would require a bottle of holy water to get out of. He needn't have worried. I never wanted to get into another situation like that.

Derol Pavey was different, though. He wasn't a ghost or a phantom, or even a shadow man. Derol was a real person. He was just having trouble speaking for himself. I thought it was the least I could do to lend him my voice. No big deal. Right?

5

Billy Bob was first at the table. Since football season started, his appetite had gone into overdrive. His mom had packed two sandwiches, an apple, chips, a couple of Twinkies, and he'd bought two pints of chocolate milk.

"Mmmph," he said in greeting. I arrived before Jase for a change.

"Hi," I said. I sat down across from him and opened my own pint of milk. I'd bought my lunch in the cafeteria. I picked up my fork and dug into a Frito pie, glad I didn't bring a lunch. Gramps must have known what was on the menu today. It was one of my favorite school lunches.

In moments, Jase was coming across the patio. No wonder I'd beaten him to the table—Frito pie was one of his favorites, too. His tray held two pies in their little red and white-checkered paper bowls, a couple of milks, and two large peanut butter cookies. I was pretty sure one of the cookies was for me. I never got dessert, but Jase always got an extra in case I wanted it. I think he was still trying to pay me back for the things the phantom pilot had done to me before we'd convinced him I was on his side.

I rubbed my forehead without thinking. A record had hit me there, but it hadn't even left a mark. I don't know why Jase still felt indebted to me.

We were chowing down when the atmosphere changed just like before. I looked up to see Derol Pavey standing, indecisively, just outside the patio doors. He had his own tray and was scanning the patio tables, looking for a place to sit.

Without thinking, I flung up my hand. "Derol," I called. "Sit with us."

Jase and Billy Bob looked at me as if I'd lost my mind. Maybe I had. Derol hesitated as if he thought it was a joke. Probably thinks I'm going to make fun of him or something.

Jase stood up, towering over everyone around us. "Yeah," he echoed. "Come sit with us."

I was so happy I think I blushed. Billy Bob finally seemed to grasp what was happening. He scooted to the end of his bench —all the tables on the patio were picnic tables—so that Derol would have room to sit. Jase sat back down beside me when he saw that Derol was headed our way.

The silence on the patio slowly broke and knots of people here and there began to chatter again. I let out the breath I was holding, but in the back of my mind I was thinking, Please don't fling your tray, please don't fling your tray...

Derol appeared to be walking on thin ice as he made his way across the patio toward our table. His hands were grasping that tray like it was made of gold.

"Hi," I said when he got close enough. "We've got plenty of room here." I made sure there was no mistaking our intentions. I could just imagine the things going through his mind.

He set his tray on the table and carefully slid in beside Billy Bob. "Thanks," he whispered. His hands were shaking so badly they were practically vibrating as he picked up his fork and began to stab at his Frito pie.

"I'm Stevie," I said, poking my fork into my own pie. "This is Jase, and the guy beside you is Billy Bob."

Derol jerked his head up and down in his version of a nod. "This is good," he said softly. "I've never had it before." His voice was musical. It had sort of a lilting quality to it. Maybe it was the Filipino accent.

"Glad you like it," I said, to keep the conversation going. "Are you and your folks getting settled into Crossroads?"

I looked up when Derol didn't answer. He was holding his fork near his mouth, but it was clear something else was going on. His eyes were squinching open and shut so quickly and so forcefully that it was making his entire face crinkle and relax, crinkle and relax, over and over.

Jase looked at me and I looked at Billy Bob and we all looked at Derol. He obviously wasn't in control anymore. Oh, no. What should we do? My first instinct was to try to put his hand down, the one that was holding the fork loaded with Frito pie. Then I recalled how he'd freaked out when Mrs. Flint had taken hold of his arm so I tried a different approach.

"Derol?" I made my voice as calm as possible so as not to attract the attention of the students sitting nearby.

He didn't reply. I saw his lips tremble in between squinches.

"Is there anything I can do?" I could feel Jase tense beside me. Billy Bob was tearing into his Twinkies like there was no tomorrow. But he was watching Derol's hands to see what he was about to do.

"Erf?" Derol said quietly. "Erf, erf?" He was doing everything in his power to control himself. But his hand was beginning to jerk.

Uh oh. Here it comes. My heart felt like it was going to explode in my chest. I tried to think of what my Gramps would do to minimize the damage, 'cause I knew if Derol started twirling and barking all heck would break loose. I was afraid if stuff started flying there would be an all out food war like last year when Dina and her sister came to school mad and dumped their milks on each other. Things had gotten wild that day. I had crawled under one table, and Jase had squeezed under another. Billy Bob had gotten hit with a blob of macaroni and cheese and got a week's detention for throwing it back into the fray. Poor Billy. Maybe that's why he was looking a little panicky now.

"Unnh," Derol said. "Uhh—" His eyes were darting back and forth in their sockets, his hand was slowly—jerkily—sinking to the table.

"Good," I whispered. "You're doing great..."

The metal fork suddenly clattered to the table and the bite of Frito pie plopped onto the ground. Derol was smiling. He'd got the fork back to the table before it flew through the air.

I felt like clapping. Jase gave him a quick thumbs-up, and Billy Bob tore the cellophane wrapper off his second Twinkie and laid one of the golden bars in front of Derol. It was like a trophy or something.

"New medicine," Derol said. His face was still squinching, but it was slower, and his eyes weren't darting anymore. That had been pretty freaky.

"Our teacher told us you have something called Tourette Syndrome," I said.

Stupid me! The squinching speeded up again. It was joined by a head jerk. I saw him flatten his hands out on the table as he took one slow deep breath after another.

"I'm sorry." I knew that sounded lame, as if sorry would help, but I didn't know what else to say. "It's okay. We don't care." Darn, that didn't sound right either. As if he was defective and we were simply accepting him.

"Hey," Jase's voice was deep and kind of loud. "You got a bike, Derol?"

"Uhhn—" He was trying to respond. His long-fingered hands were almost digging holes in the tabletop.

"'Cause I was thinking, if you weren't doing anything after school, you could ride over to the drugstore with Stevie and me."

I noticed he didn't look at Derol when he spoke to him. He simply waited for an answer, or at least a noise of some kind. This was the first I'd heard about a trip to the drugstore, but I wasn't about to say otherwise. I ate the rest of my lunch and tried to pretend Derol's head wasn't jerking back and forth like a...like a swish broom in the hand of a madman. Suddenly, something about his movements reminded me of the horrific dream and the girl in my bathroom mirror.

My stomach clenched, and I had a moment of pure panic. Am I going to lose my lunch right here in front of God and everybody? That made me forget about Derol completely.

Of course, that's when Sandy Morrison strolled by with his buddy, Fred. "Oughta be in a home," he said, his voice even deeper and louder than Jase's. Although he appeared to be talking to Fred, the burn was intended for Derol, and probably for us, too. Billy squirmed on his seat as if he would rather be somewhere else. I wondered what would happen in football practice later.

"Some people are just rude," I said to the air. "Think they're better than everyone." Apparently my voice carried better than I thought, because all of a sudden, Sandy turned and stared right at me. I wanted to shrink into my jacket and disappear, but that wasn't an option. So I stuck my tongue out at him. I didn't mean to, it just happened. Maybe I've got Tourette's or something. Can't control my own actions.

Jase almost fell off the bench he was laughing so hard. But Billy wasn't laughing, and neither was Sandy. And Derol, well, as soon as the focus was off him, he eased up and stopped squinching. His head still jerked slightly, though.

"I think I just made a mortal enemy," I muttered.

Fortunately, the lunch bell rang and Sandy turned to go inside.

Well, I thought, I would certainly have plenty to write to Karla in my next letter.

We gathered up our trays and from the corner of my eye I saw Derol stuff the Twinkie into his mouth. I think he was grinning. It was sort of hard to tell through all the yellow cake and white filling covering his teeth. Billy Bob looked stunned as we hurried into the cafeteria, stacked our trays, and dropped our forks into the bucket of soapy water at the end of the counter. His face looked like he was thinking, "What just happened?"

Jase dropped his fork into the bucket and nudged Billy. "See ya after practice."

Billy nodded.

Derol wandered around behind us, copying our movements. That's when I realized this was the first time he'd lasted through a lunch period. "You know where your next class is, Derol?"

He jumped as if my words had goosed him in the ribs. "Umm, yeah. Choir."

I hoped my face wasn't as easy to read as Billy Bob's, 'cause I wasn't just stunned, I was flabbergasted. Then I thought, well, his voice is quite musical. Why not choir?

"You're in luck," I said. "That's exactly where I'm headed." I gave Jase a little wave. "See you in English."

Jase nodded. "Take it easy, Derol." Then he smiled. "It's really not such a bad place when you get used to it."

Derol looked at him with wide eyes, but he didn't reply. He followed me toward the choir room. It was my absolute favorite place in the world except for the public library, my own front yard, and the band hall.

The choir room had an atmosphere. I don't know what it was exactly. It was as if the air inside that room was charged with possibility. Everyone was there because they loved to sing, and having a bunch of people together just because they like the same thing, well, that made it special. Not even the band hall had quite the same vibe. Folks in band didn't have to be musical, not completely. They could be good marchers, like me. Or they might simply have a flair for rhythm, the way Jase did. There were lots of different reasons to join the band, but only one reason to join the choir.

I think Billy Bob felt the same way about football. He couldn't wait to get out on the practice field each day, and on game days he was practically on another planet until time for kickoff.

Mr. Morrow always came in singing. Then he went directly to the piano and started playing the scales. No one had to be told what to do next. We all took our places on the risers and started singing. It was a very loose class. No one acted up or caused trouble.

When Mr. Morrow saw Derol, he executed a little bow. His fingers never left the piano keys. Instead, he sang, "I heard you were coming, Mr. Derol Paveeeey. Welcome, welcome, welcome to our schoooool. Glad you joined the choir-r-r-r." All of this was being sung to the tune of the scales we were practicing, but it wasn't weird. Mr. Morrow sang stuff to us all the time. It gave us the confidence to sing right back to him when it was our turn. "I don't know for certaaain," he continued to sing. "But I'll bet you're a tenor-r-r-r."

Derol grinned, and then the strangest thing happened. He began to sing back to Mr. Morrow. "You are correct, siiir," he sang. "I was tenor in my old schoooool. Where should I stan-n-d?"

Mr. Morrow's face beamed as he sang, "Tenors raise your ha-a-a-a-nds."

It was just that simple. Derol took his place among the

tenors off to my right, and he didn't jerk or twitch or fling anyone anywhere. Singing was like a magic spell or something. Of course, he did sway a bit. But it was choir—who didn't sway?

6

After choir, it was back to English with Jase. When I got there, he was waiting at the door. His face was as open as the novel we were reading. He couldn't wait to hear how choir had gone with Derol.

"It was amazing," I said, as we took out seats at the back of the room. "He sang every note with hardly a waver. Best of all, he has a great voice."

"Wow."

Jase seemed less than dazzled.

"Isn't that wonderful?" I couldn't keep the excitement out of my voice. I loved singing and I loved the fact that Derol was so good at it. Jase didn't respond.

"What is it?" I asked, taking out my copy of The Outsiders while we waited for class to begin.

Looking away, toward the door, Jase mumbled something I didn't catch.

"What?" I leaned up to try and see his lips move.

He mumbled again.

That wasn't like Jase. I poked him in the bicep with my Bic pen. "What are you saying? I can't—" I was going to say, I can't understand you, but Mrs. Kennedy walked in followed by Amber Haynes and her cadre of cuties.

They sashayed across the room and sat in their little section in the corner, automatically turning their desks just the slightest bit so that they were sort of facing in toward each other. There were five of them, an assortment of cheerleaders, baton twirlers, and wannabees. They weren't all like Amber. In fact, most of them were very nice. But when they were around her, they sometimes forgot how nice they really were.

Jase turned back toward me and pulled out his book.

"What were you saying?" I whispered.

He just shook his head and nodded toward the front of the room where the teacher was writing a list of questions on the board. Our tests were always essay rather than multiple choice since our grammar grades came from our sentence structure within the context of our answers.

We passed our books forward and the person at the front of each row stacked them on the counter so that no one would be tempted to try to peek inside and find answers in the parts we had been assigned to read.

I was afraid I would never find out what Jase was trying to tell me after that. It sounded like you really like him. Oh well, he would tell me later if it was important. I wondered what class Derol had hurried off to. He hadn't spoken any more during choir.

The test was easy. I made an A and I was certain Jase did, too. It was sort of like singing for Derol, I suppose. If you like some-thing, it just comes more easily. After class, Jase and I were walking toward the band hall when he suddenly reached down and grasped my hand.

"You never told me any more about your dream," he said.

I looked down at our hands, and all the words left my mind. "Huh?"

He looked at our hands, too, as if he didn't know what he'd done.

"Oh, the dream," I muttered. "So much has happened today, I almost forgot."

He released his grip, and my hand fell to my side

"It has been quite a day," he replied. We saw Billy headed toward the gym where the team would go over plays and suit up to take their turn on the field in a while. I realized that I hadn't thought about Janis Joplin or Jimi Hendrix all day. I hadn't even thought about the strange mirror-girl except when Derol reminded me of her at lunch.

"You really like him, don't you?" Jase's question was tense. It didn't sound anything like his usual laid-back voice.

We were just inside the band hall, putting our books away. I unearthed my clarinet case from the cabinets. "Who? Billy Bob?" We'd just seen him in the hallway.

Jase rolled his eyes.

"You looked like Buddy there for a minute," I joked. Buddy was his horse.

"Derol Pavey," he said flatly.

I looked up, then, to see if he was trying to be funny or something. I was already so used to kids making fun of Derol, I sort of expected a joke. "Derol?"

He nodded, flipped his hair off his forehead, and shuffled his feet, widening his stance defensively.

Students were milling around, trying to push past us to the storage cabinets, talking and laughing, but we simply stood there looking at each other in an ocean of silence.

"You really like him, huh?"

Finally, it dawned on me. He was asking if I liked Derol as a boy. It wasn't so much the words he said as it was the fact that he was still standing there waiting on my answer rather than dashing to the percussion section to start pounding on the drums the way he usually did as soon as we arrived.

What could I say to that? I didn't even think of him as a boy. I didn't think of Billy Bob as a boy. In fact, I didn't think of any other boys at all. Only Jase. And he wasn't really on my boy-meter. He was just sort of...my best friend.

"Well..." I pictured Derol as he was in choir, straight black hair shiny under the fluorescents, coffee-brown eyes focused on Mr. Morrow, mouth open wide with singing, and I was surprised. He wasn't just someone with a problem. He wasn't just an underdog in need of my assistance. Nope. He was a boy, a very good-looking boy, tall and dark and exotic.

"Yes," I said honestly. "I do like him, but not like I like you." I said that last part in a hurry in case my voice betrayed me. I wanted to look up at him to gauge his reaction, but I couldn't. What if his face said something I didn't want to see?

I needn't have worried. Jase gave my arm a little squeeze, and then he turned around and practically ran to his drum section. He was smiling when I finally got up my nerve to look.

"HALDOL," Derol said when we met up at the bike rack after school. "That's the name of my new drug. It's helping a lot." His arm flung itself into the air once, and then it was still. He was swaying a bit, and his head was doing that little sideways thing, but it was cool. In a way, he reminded me of Joe Cocker, the British singer whose jerky movements onstage were as well known as his music.

Jase and I had just come in from the field where we'd prac-ticed marching. That always put us in a good mood. Now we were, apparently, on our way to the drugstore. At least that's what he'd said earlier. Of course, I'd have to stop by the Police Department and tell my Gramps. He didn't get off work for another forty-five minutes. If he got home and I wasn't there, he would be worried.

"Hey, man," Jase nodded to Derol. "Where's your bike?" He unlocked his. I unlocked mine, and we sat straddling them, waiting for Derol to speak.

Instead, he simply wagged his head back and forth. Seemed like he did better when no one actually spoke to him. He wiggled his jaw with his fingers as though he might loosen it up and let the words come out. Then he turned around in a circle. His arm flew up again.

I didn't look at Jase. I was afraid he might roll his eyes like he'd done in the band hall. What was it we'd done earlier when Derol had started to freak out? Acted like it wasn't happening?

I secured my books in my basket and pretended not to notice what was going on with my new friend. "Are we going to the music store, too?" My question was directed at Jase, but mainly I was just killing time, waiting for the Tourette storm to subside.

He shrugged. "We could just go to Dal Paso and get a Coke."

A sudden thought seized me. I'd never told Jase the rest of my dream. Yep, talking over a Coke would be good. It would take the place of my going home alone, too.

"I can't," Derol said suddenly. "I have to go. Psychiatrist." He stood still for the moment, biting the words off as if from a conversation loaf. His eyes looked a bit wild.

"Oh, okay. Maybe next time, then." Psychiatrist? Wow. I didn't even know we had one in Crossroads. I sure didn't know anyone who'd ever been to one. Especially not a kid. I hoped he didn't advertise it. Just more arsenal for the kid-cannon.

"Maybe Mama will let me ride my bike tomorrow." His face was pleasant, but it was still jerking to the side a bit. It made me wonder what his symptoms would be like if he hadn't started a new medicine.

"Maybe she will," I replied. "We ride ours everyday."

He nodded jerkily, and then ran toward a dark colored Plymouth waiting at the curb.

Jase started riding very slowly, waiting for me to catch up. The parking lot was almost empty by this time because most kids rode the bus, walked, or rode bikes like us. Not many would allow their moms to pick them up after school. It was a pride thing, I guess. We had to have some sort of independence.

The air was nice. I stopped my bike and tied my jacket around my waist. Fall in West Texas was usually warm with only a few crisp days thrown in for good measure. It might start out in the forties or fifties in the morning, and be up in the seventies or even the eighties by the time school let out. I loved it. I couldn't imagine living anywhere else, except for New York City maybe. When I was grown, which I hoped was...never.

"C'mon, Pokey," Jase called.

I grinned. He'd caught me daydreaming about New York and weather. I'll bet the trees are all red and gold in Central Park at this time of year. I gave my head a little shake—comically reminding myself of Derol. I didn't have a clue what kind of trees grew in Central Park. I'd only read about it in books, never even actually seen a picture. Might be something to look up on my next trip to the library.

Jase leaned back and crossed his arms over his chest. He was smiling, but there was something different about the way he was looking at me. I chalked it up to impatience. "I'm coming. I'm coming!" I stood up on the pedals and cranked my knees, gaining momentum as I flew past him, his face a surprised blur, and kept going. The feel of my self-generated breeze was magnificent. It blew my worries away like magic.

7

In seconds Jase caught and passed me. By the time we skidded into the PD parking lot, we were both pink-cheeked and panting. "No fair!" I scolded. "Your legs are a mile long."

"Better eat more Wheaties, shrimp." He held the door open, and we both strolled inside.

"Hey, kids," Gramps said. "What's going on today?"

"Just going over to Dal Paso to get a Coke," I replied. "Wanted you to know where I'd be." Then I was out the door and headed for my bike, hoping for a head start on the giant.

"Hey," Jase called. "You might as well wait. You know it's hopeless."

I ignored him, jumped on my Stingray, and poured on the speed. Unfortunately, I had to stop for the traffic light on the corner. He pulled up beside me and flipped his hair out of his eyes just as the light turned green. "See ya," he said, standing up on his pedals and leaving me in the dust.

The Dal Paso drugstore was almost deserted when we arrived. We got Cokes and fries, looked over the comic books, and headed for a booth.

We ate in silence, and he finally asked, "What about that dance?"

"The Halloween dance?" I stalled, trying to think of what to say without giving too much away. Of course I wanted to go with him. But I didn't want him to think I was jumping to conclusions by just assuming we'd go as a couple. I tried to play it cool. "I can't wait to go. Wonder if Derol is going?"

Oops. Wrong thing to say. Jase slid out of the booth and started toward the door. Sometimes I wished I had a brake on my mouth like the one on my bike. If I wasn't sticking my tongue out, I was spitting out the wrong words.

"Wait," I cried. I swept my napkin across the table, downed the remainder of my Coke, and started after him. And they say girls are sensitive.

In a few moments I saw him turn on 4th Street leading back toward my house. As we neared the old elementary, I remembered the little face I thought I'd seen staring out at me that morning on the way to school. What a long day it had been. That seemed like eons ago.

Apparently, Jase remembered, too. He slowed to a stop and allowed me to catch up.

"What's wrong?" I asked, as I huffed and puffed my way to where he'd stopped. I felt like the big bad wolf. My breath was short and choppy. "You mad?"

"Nah. Nothing's wrong." He kicked the ground with his heel as he spoke. He wouldn't look at me. It didn't matter. I was staring at the front of the old school. Right below the still visible letters that spelled out Central Elementary, were the wide double doors. Over all that was the curved arch that gave the entrance such an old-south elegance. Something about it triggered the memory of my swishy dream from the night before. The archway looked very familiar.

Jase stopped talking and followed my gaze. "What is it? Did you see something again?"

I shook my head. I didn't know how to describe the awful feeling of sadness that had washed over me at the sight of that tall, brick arch. "I don't know," I whispered. "I don't see anything, but I feel something."

He turned his attention completely toward the school. "You never finished telling me about your dream."

I rolled my bike back and forth gently. "There was a girl with long white hair—wild white hair—and she was standing beneath an archway just like that one."

Jase backed his bike up next to mine, but he didn't speak.

"She was swishing back and forth like a little girl's rag doll in the hands of a big mean bully." I tried to recall the details. "She was dressed in a long black dress. You know, the kind they wore a long time ago?"

"Sounds like a real nightmare," Jase said. "Did she say or do anything else?"

I shook my head. "No. But she's the same one I saw in my bathroom mirror. Instead of me looking out, it was her. And then she turned her face toward the door like she was afraid someone, or maybe something, was about to walk in."

Jase grimaced. "That's even worse than Mr. Gilpin, the phantom pilot. It would freak me out, to see someone else in my own bathroom mirror—"

He was about to say more, but at that moment we both noticed a shadow moving across the window. "Did you see that?" I whispered.

"Someone's in there," Jase replied. "C'mon!" He headed for the front of the school at warp speed. I was close behind.

8

Of course the doors were padlocked shut with a length of chain.

We stood in the coolness of the overhanging archway and pressed our faces to the filthy glass beside the thick wooden doors. It was already late afternoon, and since the sun was on the west side of the school and the front of it faced the east, it was fairly dark both inside and out.

"Can you see anything?" My heart was pumping from exertion and excitement.

"Not yet. Letting my eyes adjust." Jase cupped his hands around his face, nose pressed to the glass. "Can you?"

I hesitated. I did see something, but what was it? "Do you—"

"Hey, what's that, in the dust on the floor?" Jase asked.

"Is it footprints or something?" I smashed my face into the dirty glass even harder.

"Can't tell for certain, but it looks more like letters." His voice sounded shivery.

"You cold?" I hugged my arms to my sides. The day had taken on a chill.

Jase turned away from the window. "It's freezing." His teeth chattered. I felt my own teeth trying to mimic his.

"It is freezing." I looked around for the sunlight that had been shining over the top of the old building only moments earlier. Stepping back, I untied my jacket from around my waist and slipped my arms inside. Then I realized it wasn't cold away from the window. "C'mere. I pulled Jase backward by the arm.

He took a long step back. "Wow, it's much warmer away from the glass."

I nodded. "Just the deep shadows under the overhang?"

He looked at me closely. "Remember how I told you I would try to touch Mr. Gilpin when he was in my room at night, and my hand would go right into something cold and misty?"

"I remember. I was just sort of hoping it wasn't that..." I let my sentence trail away, afraid to complete my own thought.

Jase stepped up to the glass. His voice was gentle. "I know. You're hoping it isn't happening again, but Stevie, I think it is. I think we opened a spook-door, or maybe it was opened for us when Mr. Gilpin's plane crashed in my back yard."

"Yeah, or even before that, when you found Lady mangled beside the road." I took a deep breath and stepped back up to the thick window beside him. Sure enough, when I stared at the filthy floor, I began to make out shaky letters smeared into the dust.

The first letter was H. Then E, L, and then P. I spoke each letter out loud. When I read the last two letters, M, E, I said them all together: HELP ME.

"Is it a joke?" I whispered.

Jase looked down at the thick chain. "The doors are locked from the outside."

That gave me the creeps. "You think someone is trapped in there? Locked inside?"

"Not the way you're thinking." He shook his head sadly. "I'm afraid if anything is trapped inside this old building, it has been there for a very long time."

I leaned forward and tried to see inside the foyer without actually having to touch the glass, and that's when I noticed it, a black and white shape. It floated across the T where the foyer intersected the main hallway, and then it disappeared.

"Did you see it?" I demanded, not giving Jase a chance to answer. "Did you see that shape?" I pointed across the wide foyer. "I think it was the girl from my dream, the frothy white hair, the black dress—"

"Was she swishing back and forth?" Jase leaned into the glass again, hands cupped around his face.

And that's when she struck the glass right in front of us.

"Gad!" Jase leaped back nearly knocking me off my feet. The girl lay on the dusty floor, twisting and writhing like a fish on a hook. Her pale eyes were wild and her white skin was so completely lacking in color she was almost transparent, and her hair, that frothy white hair, looked just like cotton batting that has been yanked out of a pillow and pulled apart by quick, grasping fingers.

I thought she'd struck the glass with her forehead and maybe that's why she was flipping around like that, but then suddenly she stopped, looked directly at us, and pointed upward, to the narrow windows near the ceiling.

My heart nearly stopped when her eyes met mine. They were so pale, they were nearly colorless. Not silver the way Mr. Gilpin's eyes had been, but nearly.

I followed her finger to see what she was pointing at, but it was too dark. "What do you think she's—"

Jase took hold of my arm to shut me up.

I looked from him to her again, and I saw why he'd wanted me to stop talking.

She was gone. Where she'd been lying on the floor, there

was nothing. The dust wasn't even disturbed. The HELP ME letters were still visible.

"I don't understand," I said. "I know she was there."

"Of course she was there," Jase agreed. "Just like Mr. Gilpin was there, when he wanted to be." He looked into my eyes to make sure I was following him.

My voice was small. "Another ghost?"

Jase just continued to stare into my face. He was holding onto my upper arm with one hand.

I glanced back into the gloom, but there was nothing to see. "How come the dust isn't all messed up where she fell?"

He turned loose of my arm and leaned back toward the glass. "I don't know. Maybe it really isn't even messed up where she wrote the letters either. Maybe she just showed us those words the way she showed us herself." We were both staring inside again, but now the light was dimmer and try as I might, I couldn't even see to the T intersection anymore.

Just as we turned to go, Jase suddenly reached out and gave the stout chain a hearty shake making it rattle loudly. The sound was startling in the silence. It made me jump and at the same time it drove home the fact that what we'd seen wasn't natural. It was supernatural.

"Before we leave, let's check out the other doors. Make sure there really isn't anyone else. Or a way for them to get in."

Jase's voice sounded determined, so I didn't argue. But in the back of my mind I was thinking, what if we do find an open door? What then? Go inside? I pushed that thought away. Cross that bridge if we come to it.

Jase was already around the corner of the building, examining every window, testing every pane of glass. "The only ones I can't reach are those up there, above the main doors, and the same ones here above the side doors." He looked up. The sun was getting very low in the sky and the panes of glass were painted the colors of a desert sunset.

"I think those are called transom windows," I said. "The ones above the doors, I mean." I'm not sure where I learned about transoms, but that wasn't surprising. I read all the time, everything that crossed my path. Things were always occurring in my brain without my knowing how they got there. Gramps once said he thought I read even in my sleep.

"Yeah," Jase agreed. "I've heard of those. But even if they are unlocked, no one could get there. And if they did, so what?" He shrugged. "There'd be no way to get down from the outside. Must be a fifteen foot drop to the floor."

I nodded. I wasn't really listening. I was too busy peering into every glass surface we passed, trying to—but hoping I wouldn't—see if the girl would show herself again.

"Should we report it?" I asked as we tried the last door, the one on the side of the building.

"I'll bet this was the kitchen," Jase said, shaking yet another rattling chain. "These doors are metal whereas all the others have been wooden."

"Should we?" I asked again. I felt like he was ignoring me. Hoping I wouldn't ask the question again.

"Report her, you mean?" His face was solemn.

I nodded, gaze on the ground as we made our way back to our bikes.

"What would we say? We saw someone who was there one moment and gone the next?"

"I don't know." I couldn't erase the Help Me words from my mind. "What if she's real, though? And we just, I don't know, didn't see her get up and run off?"

Jase stopped in his tracks and turned me to face him. "I never took my eyes off her after she fell to the floor." His voice was kind but firm. "She wiggled around, then she pointed up at the windows before she vanished. Just like Mr. Gilpin did in the barn that day."

I sucked in my bottom lip and held it between my teeth. It wanted to tremble again. It wanted to make me cry. Jase was acting so grown up, and I felt like such a scared little kid. "Okay," I whispered. "Okay. I trust you." I looked at him. "I just can't believe it. I never thought we'd go through something like that. Again."

"I know," he said. "Me, either. If I hadn't seen it with my own eyes, I wouldn't believe it at all."

We walked back to our bikes in silence.

"Did you notice that last chain and lock?" Jase was almost talking to himself, as if he was trying to figure something out.

"You mean on the metal doors?"

He nodded absently. "Yeah. Something about that lock was different." He stopped in his tracks and turned around. "Hang on a minute. Be right back." He took off at a sprint.

I stared after him for a second before following slowly. "What is it?" I called.

Jase was examining the lock that held the chain in place across the metal doors. "Look at this."

"Yeah?" I didn't see anything wrong with it.

"It's new," he said, cradling the shiny lock in his palm. "All the other locks are old and kind of rusty looking. But this one looks brand new."

A weird feeling crept over me again. "What do you think it means?"

Jase let the lock down gently. The chain didn't even rattle. "I don't know," he said. "But it's kind of odd, isn't it?"

I nodded and turned toward our bikes. "I've got to get home. It'll be dark in a few minutes."

"Yeah, I'm just going to go with you, if you don't mind." He didn't look at me. "Just to make sure your Gramps is home and everything, you know."

That kind of surprised me. What was he worried about? "You think she's in my bathroom mirror, again?" I pedaled slowly. "How can she be there and here?"

Jase rode along beside me, his long frame dwarfing the lean lines of his old bike. "I've been wondering the same thing," he admitted. "Remember how we decided Lady was the link that allowed her master, Mr. Gilpin, to materialize at will when she was around?"

"Ye-e-s." I twisted the end of my braid and tucked it into the corner of my mouth nervously. "But Lady went with her old master and mistress when they moved on."

"Right." Jase seemed to be thinking on the fly. "So what is the conduit here? Is it you, somehow?" He looked at me so searchingly it made me feel like a Christmas turkey trussed up on a platter.

"It isn't me!" I squeaked. "Why would it be me?"

Jase laughed self-consciously. "No, you're right. Of course, it isn't you. Why would it be? But there has to be some sort of connection."

"Yeah." I spat the end of my braid out, finally accepting the fact that we had another ghostly mystery on our hands. "Maybe she was a student. Do you know when the old school closed?"

"Easy to find out," he said.

"My mom went there," I said quietly. "That couldn't be the connection. Could it?"

Jase stopped riding and put one foot on the ground. The other was still on his bike pedal. "I think my mom went there, too," he said. "So maybe both of us are the connection, but why now? After all this time?"

I didn't have an answer for that. I didn't have a clue.

We just stood there in the middle of the intersection of 4th and Main, gaping at each other like two bunnies caught in the shine of a full hunter's moon.

9

We rode the rest of the way home in near silence. Once we got to my house and Jase saw that my Gramps was there, he took off. His house was on the northern edge of town so he had to really book to make it before dark.

"Don't look in the mirror," he said as he turned his bike toward his own home.

"Surrre," I said sarcastically. Apparently boys had completely different grooming habits than girls. I mean, how would I wash my face or comb my hair, or even brush my teeth without looking in the mirror? I watched him ride away, and as he grew smaller and smaller, something inside me lurched. What would I do if I ever lost Jase? It was so easy to lose people. What would I do if something happened to him, or my Gramps? I'd already lost my parents and my Gran, and for all intents and purposes, Karla.

I ran up the porch steps, flung open the screen door, and sang out, "I'm home."

"Just in time for pork chops and gravy," Gramps said. "Hot

biscuits need some butter. They're just canned, but they'll do for now."

I rushed over and gave him a huge hug around his middle.

"Glad to see you, too, Stevie-girl." There was a smile in his voice. "Everything all right?"

"Fine," I replied. "Just glad to be home."

We ate supper in the living room on our old metal TV trays while we watched the news about the war. We always watched for Karla's dad whenever pictures of soldiers came on, but we never saw him. Now that Jase and I were friends, I also kept a look out for his brother, Rusty. I'd never met him, but I'd seen a picture of him in his uniform on Jase's living room wall. He looked just like Jase except taller, with rusty-red hair and a serious expression.

"I guess we won't ever see them," I lamented, clearing the dishes away.

"Might not," Gramps agreed, "but it doesn't hurt to watch and hope." He picked up his newspaper and looked at a headline or two. "I think the protesters are getting more coverage than the soldiers." He studied a picture that had been reprinted from last year. It showed a poster of a pile of dead people on a dirt road somewhere in Vietnam. Most were women and children. Some were babies. The caption on the poster read "And babies?" Then at the bottom, in answer to the title caption, it said, "And babies."

I guess Gramps hadn't realized I was looking over his shoulder. "What is that?" I cried. "What happened to those people?"

"Ahh," Gramps folded the paper together quickly. "I didn't mean for you to see that, kiddo."

"But what happened?" I couldn't get the image out of my head.

Gramps stopped rattling the newspaper in his attempt to refold it. "War, sweetie. That's war."

"Why babies? I don't understand." I felt sick to my stomach.

Sitting down and pulling me onto his knee as if I were still a little child, Gramps explained how our soldiers had killed those people because their superior officers had told them to, and because they thought someone from that village was hiding enemy soldiers. "It was a crime of revenge and stupidity, and a tragedy that is still being investigated," he said. "Even in war, some things should not be allowed."

I tried to understand what he was telling me, but it was too difficult. I didn't understand why we sent men halfway around the world to fight and die in the first place.

Gramps kissed me on the head and I reveled in the smell of his Old Spice aftershave. "Don't try to understand it now," he said. "Just be aware that if you think something is wrong, trust your instincts. Stand up for yourself and others, even if no one stands up with you."

I nodded, hot tears smarting behind my eyelids. I was seeing the dead babies and children in the black and white picture, but I was thinking of Derol Pavey and how frightened he looked every time he walked into a classroom. As if he knew someone was just waiting to embarrass him in some way.

That also made me think of Anna Packett, the chubby girl in my social studies class. I didn't know her, but I knew that look in her eyes when she entered the classroom or walked down the hall trying to stay out of everyone's way. That look was just like Derol's. Why had I never noticed it before? Just because I didn't join in the teasing didn't mean I couldn't hear people calling her things like tubby and Moby.

After I finished the dishes, while Gramps was taking his bath, I quietly unfolded the newspaper and read the article that accompanied the shocking photo. It told about a place called My Lai, a village in Vietnam. It went on to describe the horrific massacre that had occurred there. I refolded the paper wishing I had taken Gramps's advice and left it alone.

I felt even worse than before, especially after reading that one of the men who finally put a stop to the killing, helicopter pilot Hugh Thompson, had been called to Congress and was reprimanded for telling the American soldiers he would shoot back if they didn't let him rescue the handful of terrified villagers who were still alive.

Is that what Gramps meant about standing up for what was right, even if you were standing alone? I mulled it over as I settled down to review the chapters we'd been assigned to read in The Outsiders. Jase and I had already read the whole book, but I didn't feel right unless I reviewed the assigned chapters. Besides, I had to do something to get my mind off that horrific photograph.

By the time I went in to get ready for bed, I had totally forgotten about the girl in the schoolhouse. Then I walked into the bathroom and looked in the mirror to take down my braid.

She was standing there, looking out at me as if she'd just been waiting. I inhaled sharply and my flight instinct kicked in. I was almost out the door when I recalled how frightened I'd been of the phantom pilot the first time I'd seen him.

Straightening my shoulders, I put both my hands against the doorjamb and forced myself to slowly turn back around. She was still there, but she was beginning to twitch. I watched her for a second. She appeared to be trying to focus on me, but her eyes kept rolling back in her head. That was awful. Her entire eyeballs looked white when they rolled upward like that.

I closed my own eyes. My knees were trembling the way they did when I had to do an oral report in front of the class. I locked them together to force them to stop shaking. "Hey," I whispered, not wanting Gramps to hear me and wonder whom I was talking to in the bathroom.

When he'd first encountered the phantom pilot, Jase had tried to tell his dad, but his dad had scoffed at him and called him a sissy for being afraid of a bad dream. I didn't want to take the chance of that happening with my Gramps. Not that he would ever call me a sissy or anything like that. He might get that funny look on his face, though. The one adults sometimes get when they don't really believe what you're saying, but they go along pretending they do, just to humor you.

All right, I thought. That's enough being scared to look in my own mirror. "Hey, little girl..." I opened my eyes. She was staring straight at me.

She was so strange looking I could hardly make my eyelids stay open. "What is it?" I whispered, my voice squeaking again. "Why are you in my bathroom?"

The girl just stood there, twitching and rolling her eyes, and then she disappeared, just like before. I actually ran over to the mirror to see if she'd fallen to the floor like in the schoolhouse, but of course, you can't see behind a reflection.

I stood for a few seconds, waiting to see if she'd reappear. When she didn't, I took a quick bath behind the closed curtain. That made me even more nervous, not knowing if she was standing there. Vulnerable. That's the word that came to my mind. I felt extremely vulnerable.

For one stomach-churning second, I was positive I could see her shadow moving about on the other side of the blue-ocean curtain. I wrapped the towel around me and yanked it open. There was nothing there. We've got to get this thing figured out, I thought. Or I'm going to be afraid to go to the bathroom alone.

That night, it took forever to go to sleep. I finally took my transistor radio and stuck it under the edge of my pillow. The reception was so spotty that it was more annoying than comforting. I read about Amelia Earhart for a bit, and that helped a little. Every once in a while my eyes would stray to the bedroom door. Did I hear something in the bathroom? Something, or someone, moving around, twitching back and forth, trying to break free of the confines of the mirror?

At some point, I finally got up, closed my bedroom door, and stuck my desk chair under the knob. If Gramps tried to come in and wake me in the morning, and he couldn't get in, what would I say? I fell asleep with that little problem chasing itself around and around in my head like a dog with a flea on its tail.

At dawn, the nightmare woke me and I sat bolt upright with a scream echoing in my mouth. Had I let it out? I listened quietly for several seconds, but there were no heavy footsteps in the hall. Gramps would've been in here by now if I had actually screamed. It must've been a dream-scream.

I rose and crossed the room as silently as possible in order to remove the chair from under the knob. The dream had been almost the same as before, the girl swishing back and forth in front of me with her wild hair and pale eyes standing out bizarrely against that solid black dress. Only there was a differ-ence this time. Right before I awoke, I saw the girl fall to the floor just as she'd done in the schoolhouse. And just like in the schoolhouse, she had continued to flip and flop and twitch as though she were in the throes of an epileptic seizure or some-thing. The fact that my dream was almost identical to the episode in the school seemed significant somehow. I thought that might be a clue of some sort. I couldn't wait to tell Jase and get his perspective.

First, I had to get dressed and out of the house without looking into any mirrors. Don't think I want to see me, anyhow. Probably look like some sort of phantom, due to lack of sleep. I pulled a long sleeved shirt over my head, slipped on another pair of blue jeans, and walked into the bathroom with my gaze cast toward the floor.

I hurriedly splashed water on my face, used the toilet,

grabbed my toothbrush and hairbrush, and high tailed it back to my bedroom. I had a mirror over my dresser, but I didn't look there, either. I wasn't taking any chances. Putting on my socks and shoes, I heard Gramps beginning to move around in his bedroom down the hall.

Letting out a sigh of relief, I glanced up to check the time on the round, silver, alarm clock, and there she was in the old-fashioned mirror above my dresser. My hand flew to my mouth to stifle an exclamation of fear.

"Stop scaring me," I hissed. "What do you want me to do?" I was beginning to get angry.

Her eyes rolled back until only the whites were visible. Then she began to shiver, her head flopping toward her shoulder as though her neck was broken.

"Oh, crud..." Before I could say more, Gramps appeared in my doorway.

"You okay, Sprout? You look pale." He moved across the room to where I was sitting, in shock, on the edge of my bed, one shoe on and one shoe off. He touched me under the chin, tilting my head back gently. "You gettin' sick?"

I shook my head and smiled to let him know I was all right. At the same time, I was trying to look around him to see if the girl was still in the mirror.

"I'M OKAY, GRAMPS." I pulled on my other shoe. "I just didn't sleep very well." I stood and gave him a brief hug, peering into the mirror at the same time. She was gone, thank goodness. "How'd you sleep?" I was pretty good at changing the subject when it needed changing.

"I slept just fine," he said. "How about some flapjacks for breakfast this morning? Or oatmeal?"

"Flapjacks." I laughed. He knew I didn't like oatmeal. "I'll get them started." I made my way down the hall, hugging the wall on the opposite side across from the open bathroom doorway.

Jase showed up at his usual time, but he surprised me by accepting a flapjack. He even ate it the same way I did, spread all over with peanut butter and rolled up like a skinny burrito.

This time, I'd thought ahead. After Gramps left and I'd cleared the table and finished washing the dishes—Gramps had done all except for my plate and glass—I pulled my toothbrush out of my pocket and proceeded to brush right there at the kitchen sink. "Don't look," I instructed Jase, who was grinning sardonically.

"I'm not," he said, peeking at me between splayed fingers.

I flipped water at him and he turned around and began to read the newspaper comics, the funny pages as Gramps called them. Jase was a big fan of Dick Tracy and Charlie Brown.

After I'd brushed and rinsed, I grabbed my jacket and books and out the door we went.

"You didn't want me to check the mirror this morning?" he asked as we began to ride.

"I saw her already. She was in the bathroom mirror last night, and then she came into my bedroom mirror this morning." I tried to sound nonchalant since Jase had the mistaken idea that I was sort of brave anyhow. I didn't want to let him down. "So, what do you think we should do? To get rid of her I mean?" The weather was golden fall again. It was my favorite time of year, besides spring. I zipped my jacket securely against the breeze.

"We have to find out what she wants," he replied. "But how are we going to do that?"

With the phantom pilot, we'd had no choice. He had demanded we pay attention. Come to think of it, this little girl was becoming pretty demanding as well.

"We have to communicate with her," I answered Jase. "I don't see how we can, though. Every time I see her, she has some kind of horrible fit and falls down on the floor. How can we communicate with her when she does that?" I tossed my braid over my shoulder and pulled my hood up. The wind was getting chillier every day. Soon, it would be Halloween and time for the dance.

"I've got an idea," Jase said, cruising along beside me at turtle speed. "I asked my mom last night if she remembered your mom from their days at Central Elementary."

He had my full attention. Any mention of my mom, or even my dad, made me feel kind of hollow inside. I missed her. I thought I should miss him, too, only I didn't know him well enough for that. "What'd she say?" My words were sticky, as if they were coated in the peanut butter I'd just had for breakfast.

"She asked me what your mom's name was back then." He whacked his forehead in mock-exasperation, as if he should have known she would ask that.

"Oh, it was Hines before she married my dad. Her name was Avis Hines." I smiled to myself, remembering how my mom hated her given name. "But everyone called her by her middle name, Ora."

Jase nodded solemnly. I think he understood about my mom. "Okay, I'll tell her tonight. Avis Ora Hines."

My chest felt tight; as if my breath was sticking the way my words had done earlier. I quickly changed the topic. "So, why do you think this girl won't come right out and show herself to us like the pilot, Mr. Gilpin, did?"

Jase thought for a moment. "Well, she sorta did, in the old schoolhouse."

"Not really. She was behind glass again, just like she always is when she's in my mirror...er...mirrors." We were almost to the old school. We didn't have time to check it out now, but the idea of those two words smeared into the dust made me wish we did have time. Maybe we could go again after school. I was about to ask Jase if he thought we should, when he said:

"Hey, maybe she's just shy, you know, like Derol. I mean she is kinda freaky looking and all." His cheeks reddened when he said that. That's what I found so endearing about Jase. He didn't even like to speak ill of a ghost.

"Maybe you're right," I agreed. "And that's why it's taken her so long to contact someone to help her. Wonder what she needs help with?"

"To get to the other side, maybe. I mean she is just a kid." Jase shrugged casually, as if helping a spirit move on was nothing more than holding the door open for me to walk into class.

10

W e locked our bikes in the rack and headed into school. I glanced back to see if Derol had ridden his bike today, but there were several others, and I couldn't be certain.

"C'mon," Jase said. "We don't want to be late."

Just inside the doorway, Jase stopped. "Let's go by the old school after Mr. Pearcy's place this afternoon."

"Okay." I'd forgotten it was cleaning day. Jase had promised to clean out the gutters, too. Fall leaves and all that.

"And, Stevie..." His voice was thoughtful.

"Yeah?" I looked up just as he flipped his hair back. Sign of nerves. "What's up?"

He was standing in front of the Halloween Dance poster again. "We don't have to go in costume," he said. He looked at me seriously and the world went away for a moment. "Just as long as we go together."

I think I gulped. Darn sticky words wouldn't come out again. "Uh, okay." Geez. Witty today. "I'd like to dress up, though. It'll be fun."

He tweaked my braid, and the spell was broken. Thank goodness. I couldn't have survived much longer without air.

Holding the door open, as always, we walked into home-room and were surprised to see Derol already there. And wonder of wonders, he even lifted one hand in a half-wave. At least I think it was intentional. With Derol, it was hard to tell. I waved back, just in case.

Mrs. Flint came in carrying the attendance roll and she also appeared surprised—but pleased—to see Derol in his seat. I was so glad when I saw her pick up a pencil and put a check mark on the roll. I was certain she was saving him the anxiety of waiting to hear his name called.

Maybe the little phantom girl was just shy. If just answering roll call could produce such stress in Derol, what must it be like for her, all alone in an abandoned schoolhouse?

I wanted to tell Jase what I was thinking, but it was too late. Sandy and his crowd were coming in, and they did like to make an entrance. Even from my seat two rows over, I could sense Derol tightening up. They really made him nervous. Heck, they made me nervous and I wasn't even the new kid.

"Come to order, class," Mrs. Flint said. After the morning announcements, she began to call the roll like always. When she got to Derol's name, she simply smiled at him, skipped it completely, and moved on to the next person. Nicky Peterson. He was here, too. I loved Mrs. Flint for that, and even though it was such a small thing, it was so perceptive of her. It was more than most teachers did to put someone at ease, that's for sure.

I saw Derol visibly relax once his name wasn't called, but then I saw something pass across Sandy's face that really made me uneasy. It was as if he didn't like Derol to be relaxed. As if he'd been hoping for some more excitement like yesterday and the day before.

Thankfully, Mrs. Flint had a handle on things. She didn't

give anyone a chance to get out of line. I tried not to stare at Derol, but he was sort of in my line of sight, my peripheral vision at least, and I noticed his leg jumping continuously. His head was still doing the sideways jerk, too. Apparently the leg thing was bugging him. Every few moments, he would smash down on it with both of his palms in an effort to still the jumping.

Lunchtime came around quickly. Social studies went by in a blur because I couldn't seem to stop doodling sketches of the little girl in the margins of my notebook. It was as if she wanted me to become obsessed with her, and it was working. I could hardly think of anything else. I did make it a point to smile and speak to Anna Packett when she walked by, though.

Billy Bob was already at the table when Jase and I arrived. Jase had been waiting for me outside the cafeteria doors with a tray of food in his hands. I had brought my lunch in one of the little brown bags that I preferred.

Together, we headed toward our picnic table where Billy was sitting with his back to us. I was about to ask Jase if he'd seen Derol. I hoped he was brave enough to sit with us again. Then I saw Billy Bob's face. One eye was black and blue, and the skin was shiny and swollen. It looked like it would split open like a bad melon if you touched it wrong.

"What happened?" My voice was incredulous. I paused with one leg halfway over the concrete bench.

Jase paused, too. "What the..."

Billy wagged his head back and forth gingerly. "Ain't nothin'. Caught an elbow in the eye at practice yesterday." He stuffed another bite of Salisbury steak in his mouth, followed by a huge chunk of bread.

"An elbow did that?" I didn't mean to sound disbelieving, but wow. He'd been on the team forever, and I'd never seen an injury like that. "Isn't that what helmets and face guards are for?

To prevent injuries?" I knew I should shut up, but I just couldn't seem to do that. Billy was my friend, and even though he was a tough guy on the field, in regular life, he was one of the kindest, silliest kids I knew. I didn't like to see him hurt.

Jase was quiet.

We sat down and began to eat.

"It was kind of a freak accident," Billy said. "Fred was coming in the gym door after we were finished on the field, and Sandy was jerking around pretending to be Derol, and I told him he wasn't funny. Fred turned around suddenly, and got me in the eye with his elbow." He looked up at us then, and we were treated to the full extent of his injury. The area around his eye was awful, but it was the eyeball itself that really looked bad. It looked as if he'd been crying bloody tears.

"Oh, Billy!" My mouth fell open and wouldn't seem to close.

He grinned, then winced when the grin made his swollen skin crinkle. "It looks worse than it is," he said. "The team trainer looked it over, told me to go home and put a steak on it. We only had pork chops..."

I couldn't help it. I laughed out loud. Of course, we'd had pork chops last night, too.

Jase wasn't laughing. "So you already had your helmet off, right?"

Billy nodded, but kept eating. I don't think anything interfered with his appetite.

"Fred is Sandy's best bud, right?"

Billy shrugged. "So?"

I saw what Jase was getting at. "You had just told Sandy to stop making fun of Derol?"

"Are you sure it was an accident, Bill?" Jase's voice was neutral.

"'Course it was," Billy answered. "I've been friends with Fred and Sandy all my life." He took a swig of milk, draining one pint and immediately opening another. "'Sides, he wasn't really making fun, just—" He didn't finish his sentence because that's when Derol came bopping in, a huge smile on his face, and headed straight for our table.

He seemed to be awfully happy about something. I had never seen him smile that way. It literally lit up his face.

Just as he got within speaking distance of us, he flipped his head sideways to get his straight black hair off his face—sort of reminded me of Jase—and that's when someone stuck out a foot and tripped him, sending his tray flying and wiping the smile off his happy, friendly face.

Jase and I both jumped up to help him. Even Billy leapt to his feet as Derol went crashing to the cement patio, arms and legs flailing, food flying to the ground in front of him.

I glanced up to see who had tripped him, but everyone that could have done it was already gone. Some kids were laughing, twittering actually, like birds on a highline wire. A few laughed out loud, but not many. Most of the students at our school were decent. But there were always a few bad apples as Gramps would say.

Derol lay absolutely still for a few seconds as Jase and I scrambled to pick up the stuff from his tray. The plate was melamine so it didn't break, and his milk was unopened so that was okay. But the Salisbury steak was ruined.

Jase leaned over to help Derol, but when he tried to grasp his arm, Derol exploded. "Leave me alone," he yelled, flailing his arms like a pinwheel as he gained his feet.

Throwing his hands up in surrender, Jase stepped back. "It's just me, Derol." He sounded very calm, thank goodness, because Derol went all to pieces, both arms flailing, brown gravy smeared on one cheek, head jerking, eyes rolling up. In truth, he was terrifying.

"Derol," I said quietly. "Please, come and sit. We'll get a new tray."

Billy jumped up and headed inside the cafeteria, but it was too late. Something had been triggered and no one knew how to turn it off, least of all Derol.

Still jerking and flailing, Derol looked at me with eyes as wild as a steer in a slaughterhouse, then he took off running. I clenched my teeth together and started after him. I didn't know where he was going, I just knew I wanted to be there in case he hurt himself or ran into the idiot who had tripped him and started this whole mess. And why did that eye-rolling thing look so familiar? What was my subconscious trying to tell me?

I couldn't stop to think about it just then, because as we approached the wide double doors, Mr. Terrance appeared. I wondered who had alerted him, or if he just knew something was going on by the sound of the voices on the patio. Billy was right behind him with another tray of food.

I held my breath as Derol got to the door. I wasn't sure if he intended to stop or go right over the top of the assistant principal. He wasn't a small boy. I was pretty sure he could take Mr. Terrance out if he wanted.

At the last second he veered off to the right, away from the doors.

"Derol, wait." I called. I didn't know what to do. I wanted to prevent more trouble, and I was pretty sure running away from the assistant principal would lead to more trouble. Lots more. Especially since he hadn't been there to see what had started it all.

Derol seemed to have gone deaf. He was around the corner of the building and out of sight before I could even think. That's when a tall streak of boy with blond hair blew past me without a word. Mr. Terrance took off. I didn't know he could get up that much speed, but in a second he, too, was around the corner and out of sight.

Billy Bob and I looked at each other in confusion. Billy shrugged and took Derol's tray to our table and sat down to eat. That's when I noticed Sandy and Missy Bridges standing off to the side, watching us without expression. When Missy saw me looking, she quickly turned her head away and said something to Sandy under her breath. I wanted to strangle her, and then I realized that they hadn't even been here when it happened. Had they? I wracked my brain trying to remember whose faces I'd seen gathered around, laughing, but instead of seeing the familiar faces of students on the patio, what came was the familiar face of the girl in the mirror, eyes rolling back in her head just like...Derol. When he was pushed too far and lost control.

I stopped in my tracks, oblivious to everyone around me, then went and sat beside Billy Bob who was quickly putting a dent in the second plate of Salisbury steak.

I was still sitting like a lump beside Billy Bob when Jase came around the corner of the building.

"What happened?" I asked.

Panting, Jase replied, "Derol is fast." He swiped a swatch of hair off his forehead like he always did. "I could've caught him though if Mr. Terrance hadn't insisted I go back to lunch."

I looked around. "So, what about Derol? Did Mr. T. take him to the office?"

Jase shook his head and slugged down the extra milk Billy had put on Derol's tray. Though the autumn weather was cool, the bright sunlight had raised a few droplets of sweat on his brow and upper lip. "Couldn't catch him."

"What?" I jumped up, ready to run and look for Derol myself.

Jase held up one finger while he finished off the milk and

wiped the mustache off with the back of his hand. When he was done, he crumpled the little paper carton and lobbed it into the nearest trashcan. Only then did he speak. By this time, I was tapping my foot impatiently.

"I stuck around, behind those sage bushes out front, to see what he would do," he said at last.

I crossed my arms over my chest, waiting. "And?"

He grinned. "Mr. Terrance pulled out his walkie-talkie and told the secretary to call Derol's mom and tell her he was on his way home...again."

"Oh, so that's what happens, huh?" I thought back to the other time Derol had gotten so upset and disappeared until the next day.

Jase nodded. "Apparently so. I heard the secretary tell him Derol's mom would call back as soon as she got home. To let them know he was there, safe and sound."

"Sounds like they've done it all before. He just freaks out and takes off running, doesn't he? Poor Derol."

"Yeah," Jase said as the bell rang warning us we had five minutes to get to our next class. "Bad thing is, he doesn't seem to realize he can't outrun himself."

Billy Bob chimed in with, "Amen to that, brother."

We all cracked up. Leave it to Billy to lighten the mood.

11

As we made our way to our next classes, Jase continued to fill me in. "Man, he was really bookin' it down the street last time I saw him. Wonder where the heck he lives?" Under his breath, to himself, he said, "Wonder if he's ever run track before?"

Track was Jase's sport. He didn't care that much for football, and he would rather be in the band with his drum at halftime, but he did love to run. He was always going on about how he was going to try out for the track team in the spring.

We were walking down the hall, me to choir and Jase to creative writing, when I suddenly recalled how Derol's wild, rolling eyes had reminded me of the girl in the mirror. "Jase."

He stopped walking. The river of students parted and went around us as he waited for me to speak. He was patience personified. I guess opposites really do attract. My patience could fit into a thimble without overflowing the rim. "Did you see Derol's face when he jumped up off the ground?"

Jase said, "Yeah, so?"

"So, did it remind you of anything? His eyes, I mean?" I

picked at the plastic coating on my notebook as I waited to hear what he would say.

"Sorta reminded me of Buddy when he thinks he hears a rattlesnake or something. His eyes go all crazy and white like that." He started to walk away again, then stopped. "Why'd you ask me that? Did he remind you of Buddy, too?"

I just shook my head. I knew what he meant. I'd seen Buddy once or twice when he thought he sensed danger. "Never mind," I said. "We'll talk later."

In choir, Mr. Morrow asked—in a singsong voice, of course —if anyone knew whether Derol was in school today. I glanced around at all the open mouths still holding the Fa in the scales. No one volunteered anything. I would've told him, but I couldn't make myself sing he flipped out at lunnnch when someone tripped himmmmm. I just couldn't.

So I stuck around after class. "Uh, Mr. Morrow?"

The music teacher looked up. He'd been gathering sheet music and organizing it into his slim briefcase. "Stevie?"

I shuffled my feet. "I just wanted to tell you, about Derol..."

He stopped organizing the music. "Yes?"

"He, umm, someone tripped him at lunch and he ran off, toward home." I started for the door, my duty done.

Behind me, I heard Mr. Morrow let out his breath. "Thank you for telling me," he said.

WE WERE FINISHED with English and headed toward the band hall, before Jase and I finally had a chance to mull over what had happened. "Do you think Derol's okay?" I asked.

Jase looked grim. "I hope so. Man, what kind of person gets a kick out of making other people feel so bad?"

I just shook my head. "Maybe we can find out where he lives

and go check on him after school, or after we leave Mr. Pearcy's house."

Jase nodded and we went on inside. In seconds, I heard him pounding the bass drum for all it was worth. I got my clarinet and took my place in the third section. I really wasn't very good.

After marching practice, we hurried to the bike rack, determined to find out what had happened. "Wait," I said. "We didn't find out where Derol lives." I turned around and headed back to the office. I didn't know if they would tell me, but Mrs. Rubinowski was usually nice, if you were nice to her first. I thought it was worth a try.

"Hey," Jase called after me.

I turned on my heel, a question in my eyes. When I saw him standing beside our bikes, I knew immediately why he had called me. There was a new bike in the rack. It was tall, like Jase's old blue one, and it was jet black. It looked new. The lock, holding the two ends of the bike chain together and looped around the rack and the bike's frame, looked even newer. It was every bit as shiny as the one we'd seen on the old schoolhouse door the day before. Another light bulb clicked on in my head.

"Derol's?" I asked, though I was certain it had to be as I recalled how happy he'd been at lunch when he was hurrying toward us, oblivious to the crowd of kids that usually terrified him. I felt sure he'd been about to tell us he had gotten a new lock and his mom had allowed him to ride to school. Another light clicked on inside my brain. This time it didn't fully illuminate the idea that tried to form there, but it pushed the shadows away somewhat, and left me with a question. If those two locks are the same, what does that mean?

"C'mon," Jase said. "I've got an idea where he might be if he isn't at home." He was holding the new lock, still attached to the two ends of the bike chain, in the palm of his hand just as he'd done at the school the night before.

"I know what you're thinking," I said. "Let me see if I can find out where he lives first. Just in case." I ran toward the school, fingers crossed in hopes that Mrs. R. was alone in the office. She was always nicest when no one else was around.

I was in luck. She was sitting at her desk like a plump setting hen.

"What can I do for you, Stevie?"

I quickly explained what had happened at lunch—though I felt certain she already knew—and then I just came right out and told her that Jase and I were going to his house to check on him. "The problem is, we don't know where he lives."

She clucked her tongue. "Now, Stevie, you know I can't give out another student's personal information,—" she surreptitiously glanced around behind her, "—but that boy does need a friend." I could see her mentally going over my entire school record in her head. I guess she decided I was trustworthy, for she finally said, "If you were to ride past the house where your friend Karla used to live, you might spy him out in the yard or something."

I started to speak, and then checked myself. I was going to tell her I would know if he had moved into Karla's house, because it was very close to my own home, but then I realized that wasn't true. I'd made it a habit to steer completely clear of my old friend's house. It made me too sad to see it without Karla's crazy tie-dyed curtains hanging in her bedroom window.

"Thank you," I said, turning for the door.

Mrs. Rubinowski clucked. "For what, dear? You didn't hear anything from me."

I smiled conspiratorially and hurried out the door into the fall sunshine.

Jase couldn't believe it when I told him where Derol lived.

"If he isn't there, we'll go straight to the old school." He gestured toward the bicycle lock again. "That's the same brand as the one we saw yesterday."

I filed that bit of information in my head, and we took off toward Mr. Pearcy's house.

As soon as we got there, Mr. Pearcy gave us chocolate chip cookies and milk. He was proud of himself for baking them all on his own. They were good, too. I called my Gramps to let him know I was where I was supposed to be, and he told me to come straight home after we were done.

I took a deep breath and related the events of the day to him in a rush. "So is it okay if we go over to Derol's house and check on him before coming home?" I asked.

"Of course," he said. "But if he isn't there, come on home. If he is there, bring him home for supper. I'd like to meet that boy."

Good old Gramps.

"I sure will," I said. I hung up the phone, and turned to see Jase and Mr. Pearcy staring at me.

"If you kids need to go check on your new friend, go ahead," Mr. Pearcy said. "I went to the grocery store this morning and picked up some baking potatoes and ham slices. I think I can handle that on my own."

"But what about the sweeping, and the mopping—?"

"And the gutters," Jase said.

"They'll all be here the day after tomorrow when you both come back," he said. "Now, run along..."

We did. But in the back of my mind I was thinking about that dollar I would've earned. Oh well, first things first, as Gramps always said.

No one answered the door at Derol's house. It was so weird standing there on Karla's front porch again. The swing was still there, but now instead of her mother's wind chimes tinkling overhead, Derol's mother had set out pots of herbs everywhere. I reached down and pinched the tip of a small rosemary bush in a large clay pot. The musty scent invaded my nostrils and drove home the fact that Karla wasn't here, and she wasn't coming back.

I pinched off another good-sized tip and held it out for Jase to smell. I had loved rosemary ever since the Simon and Garfunkel song Scarborough Faire hit the charts.

Jase wrinkled his nose at the unfamiliar odor. "I don't think they're here. Should we try the old school?"

I hopped off the porch. I didn't like being there. It felt wrong somehow. "Yes, let's go check out that new lock on the schoolhouse door."

The school wasn't far. Was the little girl in there? Was Derol? Could they be connected somehow? It sure seemed like she had appeared about the same time he did.

We rode right up to the front doors like we'd done the day before, only this time, it wasn't quite as late and the shadows weren't quite as deep. In fact, there was still a bright glare streaking across the dirty windows. That made it even harder to see inside.

Jase put his hands around his face again, and peered inside. He motioned for me to join him. Sure enough, right there in the thick dust, for the entire world to see, were the words HELP ME!

We looked at each other and took off around the building toward the cafeteria doors where we'd seen the suspicious lock.

It wasn't there.

Jase looked at the bare door and then scratched around in the weedy grass with his foot until he found something. When he bent over to pick it up, I assumed he'd found the chain that the lock had been holding across the double doors, but when he raised up and showed me what he had, I realized it was the old, rusted lock that must have hung on the door for years—until someone came along and knocked it off somehow.

"How hard would it have been to break that?" I asked Jase as we examined it closely.

"I dunno," he admitted. "It's pretty rusty. I guess if someone hit it hard enough, with a rock or something—"

I stood still in the late sunshine, thinking. "Why would anyone want to go in there? It's so creepy."

Jase just shook his head and tossed the lock back into the weeds. "A better question is, who's in there now?" He reached out and touched the unlocked door. "And what are they doing?"

I looked behind me, suddenly certain that someone or something had crept up on us while we were examining the lock. No one was there, but the sun had disappeared and goose bumps pimpled my arms, even inside my jacket.

12

"I'm going in." Jase pulled open one of the gray metal doors. It didn't make a sound.

"How come it didn't creak?" I whispered. "It should have creaked."

Jase held his finger to his lips. "Maybe someone oiled it," he whispered.

For some reason, that did not make me feel better. Whoever was in the old building knew how to be sneaky. "I don't know about this," I said, following him inside.

The door closed behind us soundlessly.

We were in a short, dark hallway. There was a hint of sunlight filtering in from the front of the old school. We stood perfectly still, letting our eyes adjust to the gloom. The pounding of my frightened heart sounded very loud in the stillness. I wondered if Jase could hear it. As I glanced around, I realized with relief that my eyes were quickly adjusting to the gloom. The short hallway fed directly into the old kitchen with its long silver counter and empty spaces where industrial stoves and freezers once had stood. Behind the counter was a set of double doors that undoubtedly housed an extra-large pantry.

Without a word, Jase grabbed my hand and pointed at the floor. Apparently, his eyes had adjusted, too, for there on the floor were large, smeary footprints that I hadn't even noticed. Whoever made them must have been in a big hurry. It looked as if the culprit had almost lost his footing going around the counter and through the large kitchen.

"Derol?" I asked.

Jase shrugged and whispered, "Could be anyone. Let's be careful."

"I have a better idea," I said, holding on to his shirtsleeve. "Let's get out of here."

Jase was still under the impression that I was brave just because he'd seen me going in the old haunted house last year by myself. What I couldn't seem to make him understand, then or now, was that at the time I went in there, I hadn't really believed in things like ghosts and shadow people. Now, I knew better.

We took a few steps into the kitchen. "Maybe you're right," he said. "Maybe we should get your Gramps or someone."

"Now you're talking," I said, and then I froze.

Standing opposite us, on the other side of the long silver counter, was the little girl.

I tugged on Jase's sleeve and pointed.

Her pale hair was wild, her eyes were almost transparent, and her face was slack and pallid. As we watched, she began to twitch and shiver. Her black dress swayed around her as though buffeted by an unfelt breeze.

"What do you want us to do?" Jase's voice was unbelievably loud in the stillness.

The little girl didn't seem to know we were there. She twitched back and forth a few more times, her eyes rolled up and she fell down behind the counter, out of sight.

We dashed around the corner. She was nowhere to be seen. As before, the dust wasn't even disturbed.

"What now?" I whispered. "Do we keep looking?"

Jase nodded, but cocked his head. "Hear that?"

I listened closely.

I could hear someone breathing!

It sounded as if they'd taken in a deep breath, held it, and then let it out in a whoosh. This was too much. I looked at the closed pantry doors. Someone was in there. I tried to remember if I'd ever heard the little girl breathing—do phantoms breathe?

Jase held up his hand in a gesture I took to mean stay. Then he crept toward the doors as quietly as possible.

I didn't want to look. I shielded my eyes with one hand (then peeked through my fingers).

Jase reached for the old-fashioned handles, prepared to yank them both at once.

He glanced back at me, then turned and gave a tremendous pull expecting to fling them wide open. They did not budge. They were either completely stuck, or securely locked.

I clenched my teeth when he leaned down and peered into the tiny keyhole below the right-side handle. He turned back to me and gave me the universal, palms up gesture that meant he had no idea what was going on.

"C'mon," I said, trying to sound normal. "Let's just go." I had convinced myself that the breathing I'd heard was just my own or Jase's. Maybe I didn't even care anymore. Maybe I just wanted out of there.

Jase nodded and together we started back through the kitchen toward the little hallway.

I was still holding on to his shirtsleeve with one hand. My other hand was poised over my brow, ready to really shield my eyes if we ran into anything too awful to look at. I expected the little girl to appear again, in all her twitchy glory, right in front of us.

"I thought Derol was in that pantry," I murmured.

Jase nodded. Then he stopped. Directly in front of us, at the entrance to the little hallway, were more footprints in the dust. This time they led toward the outside door, the way we'd just come in. Our own footprints were stamped going the other way. These prints had not been there a moment earlier. It gave me pause to see them, as if we'd suddenly joined the host of the unseen that seemed to inhabit this place.

I clutched Jase's arm tightly. Those footprints were large. I felt, instinctively, that they belonged to Derol. But if so, why wouldn't he wait for us? Surely by now he knew he could trust us.

Jase took my hand—probably to make me stop digging my nails into his flesh. "It's okay," he said. "Whoever it was is gone."

I relaxed. If Jase said it was all right, then I believed him. I turned loose of his hand, and there was the little girl, again.

This time she stood between the door and us. She looked the same as always, but dimmer somehow. Just as I opened my mouth to speak, she disappeared. But not before motioning toward the front of the school with one pale, slender hand.

"C'mon!" Jase yanked me toward the double doors that would take us back outside.

They wouldn't open.

We looked at each other in shock.

Jase pushed them again, but nothing happened. In frustration, he placed a palm on each door and shoved them solidly, over and over. The metal doors rattled, but would not open. The sound was magnified by all the old tile and big emptiness of the hall and kitchen. I clapped my hands over my ears to shut out the reverberations bouncing off the walls.

"Someone locked us in," Jase muttered angrily. He shoved

the doors again to prove it, and a tiny strip of daylight appeared between them.

"Look." I ran my finger down the narrow slice of light. "Maybe they aren't locked. Something seems to be holding them shut from the outside, but I think it's weakening." Without a word, we put our shoulders to the doors and shoved as hard as we could.

We fell right through the doors and onto the little brick apron outside as the chain that had been looped through the door handles gave way with a clatter. It puddled into a heap on the brick. Whoever had run out a few moments earlier must've simply looped it through the door handles. The old, rusted lock was lying beside it, as if they'd stuck it through the chain ends. Thank goodness it was broken and wouldn't close all the way. The new lock was still nowhere to be seen.

Dusting ourselves off, we peered down the length of the outside wall. "What'd they do that for?" I asked. "Do you think it was Derol, trying to scare us away or something?"

Jase didn't answer. He felt around in the weeds with his foot again. "I looked for that chain when we got here, but I couldn't find it. Whoever had it must've been carrying it with them." He glanced at me. "Thank goodness they didn't have the new lock. They might have locked us in completely."

The mention of the good lock made us realize we'd left our bikes unattended at the front of the school. Anyone could have taken them. But when we rounded the corner, there they stood, just as we'd left them.

My heart loosened up a bit. "That was sort of terrifying, wasn't it?" I was speaking to myself and to Jase if he was listening. He wasn't. He was at the front windows, peering in through the glass again.

"I'm going back in," he said. "You wait out here."

"What for?" My voice showed my disbelief. I had seen enough of the inside of that school for one afternoon.

Jase pushed the hair off his forehead in exasperation. "Because if you're out here, no one can lock me in there."

"But why go in at all? Whoever was hiding obviously got out before we did."

His usually clear green eyes were dark with indignation. "Because, I'm not going to let some eerie little girl frighten me away when I think she really wants us to help her."

That's my Jase. Pride and courage all rolled into one tall, lanky package.

I took a deep breath, threw my leg over my banana seat, and prepared to wait. "Okay, I'll wait here, but if you aren't back in five minutes I'm going to get Gramps."

Jase stopped and looked at me as if he wanted to say something else, then he just shook his head and took off.

I rode my bike to the front windows under the archway, leaned over without getting off my bike, and pressed my nose to the glass. I opened my eyes as wide as possible and vowed not to cringe or jump back if the little girl appeared. In a few seconds, Jase came bounding into view. I waved heartily. I was so glad to see him. He waved back nonchalantly, crossed the foyer, and started down the hallway opposite of where the classrooms were located.

As soon as he disappeared from view, the little girl reappeared. My heart stuttered. She looked up at me with those spooky, transparent eyes, and then her head rolled to the side, her body started to twitch back and forth and then—

"What are you doing, little girl?" The voice behind me was deep and rough.

I whirled around and found myself face to face with a kid who must've been at least a senior in high school, maybe even out of high school already. He was taller than Jase, twice as wide, and his face was dark and ruddy.

"I—I was just looking around." I glanced over my shoulder, but the girl was gone. What if Jase comes back through now? Was this the person who was in the pantry? Or the one who looped the chain through the door handles?

He looked me up and down, as if taking my measure. My skin felt like it was shrinking on my body. His eyes were unreadable. "You need to go on home before you get in trouble." His voice was gruff. It convinced me he was even older than I'd first thought.

I backed up, hoping he hadn't noticed Jase's bike leaned against the pillar on the other side of the archway.

"Who does that belong to?" He jerked his thumb over his shoulder without looking.

I bit my lip and crossed my fingers behind my back. "It's my friend's. He'll be here in a second."

His red face grew even redder. "He the one's been sneaking around in there?" He pushed past me and shoved his big face up to the glass.

Please don't let him see Jase. Please don't let him see Jase. Please don't...

I said, "No, I mean, we thought we saw someone run out of there." That was pretty close to the truth. "Are you the caretaker or something?" I didn't mean that to sound sarcastic, but it sort of came out that way.

The guy turned from the glass and glared at me. Over his shoulder, I saw Jase scurry through the foyer and headed toward the kitchen and the outside door.

"Yeah," he barked. "Something like that." He started off toward the side of the building where I knew Jase would be making his exit about now. I had to draw his attention elsewhere.

As loudly as I could without actually yelling, I said, "Hey! Who's that?" And then I threw my bike into overdrive and took off in the opposite direction at top speed. Imagine my surprise when I ran almost headlong into Fred Green and his little brother, Will. They were crouched behind the scraggly bushes at the opposite corner of the building.

"Fred." I stepped on the pedals and came to a skidding halt in front of them.

He stood and raised one hand in greeting. His black hair and ruddy complexion told me right away that the big guy was his older brother. It's a wonder I hadn't noticed it right away. "Hey, Stevie, what's going on?" He tried to sound innocent, but I immediately suspected that he'd been there all along. I looked at his other brother, Will, who was just getting to his feet behind him, but he wouldn't meet my gaze. I remembered him from elementary school. He was only a year behind us, but everyone already knew his name. The Green brothers were notorious bullies. Except for the older one. I didn't know him at all. He was scary.

"What's going on?"

Relief flooded my body. That was Jase's voice. He was striding toward us from behind Fred and Will. Apparently he'd heard my crude warning and had dashed out and sprinted the other direction to come up from behind the old school as if he'd just been down the block or something. The older Green boy was slowly making his way toward us from the other side of the archway. My little ruse had worked.

"Just waiting for you, Jase." I hoped the relief wasn't as audible to them as it felt to me.

Jase grinned that slow grin that told me everything was all right. "Hey, Fred, Will." He held his hand up in greeting as he passed them, as if meeting here at the old school was just another everyday occurrence. Then he saw the other brother, and he came to a halt.

I gave him a hard look to let him know this was why I'd practically yelled out that warning. "I've got to get home," I said. "My Gramps is expecting me. You, too, Jase. You said you would help with those gutters." Okay, that wasn't exactly true. The gutters belonged to Mr. Pearcy, and that was not until day after tomorrow, but I did what I always did when I needed an excuse to get out of something uncomfortable. I fell back on the explanation that my Gramps wouldn't like it, or my Gramps needed me at home. He'd told me to do that, and it worked.

When Karla had wanted me to sneak out with her one night, I just told her I was afraid of what my Gramps would do if he found out. That wasn't really true. I was never afraid of him, just afraid of disappointing him. But it had worked. She didn't bug me about it after that, and if she had gone ahead with her plan, she never told me about it. Good old Gramps. When I confessed it to him later, after Karla had moved, he said I could make him sound as bad as I wanted. He said I could use him as an excuse to stay out of trouble any time.

Now, it seemed to work again. Jase strode past the bigger boy, slung his leg over his bike, and we took off without another word.

I had a hard time not looking over my shoulder as we rode away.

13

"Who was that guy?" I asked when I was certain we were out of earshot.

"Fred's older brother. I think his name is Ross. He's the one that got in trouble last summer for setting fires in the trashcans behind the school...twice."

We were almost to my house. "Thanks for riding home with me. You don't have to come in unless you want to."

Jase slowed almost to a stop. "We didn't find Derol, you know."

"No, but we sure found something. Fred and his brothers, the little girl again, and that breathing."

"Yeah, that breathing was weird. I wish we could have gotten that door open." He seemed to be thinking about something.

"What?" I asked as we stopped beside my front porch. I could almost see the gears spinning in his head.

Jase leaned his bike against the porch rail before he carefully spoke. "I've got to go back," he said.

I started to protest, but his next question stopped me in mid-thought.

"Does your Gramps have a screwdriver I can borrow?"

I looked around. Gramps's pickup truck was in the carport. That meant he was inside, probably watching TV or starting supper. "What are you going to do?" I asked. I didn't think I wasn't going to like the answer. In fact, I was pretty sure he was planning on going back in the school to take the doors off that pantry. "You're not really going to go back, again. Are you?" I could see that stubborn look on his face. His lips were drawn into a solid line.

He reached up and wiped the hair off his forehead. He had one foot on the bottom porch step, and one foot on the ground. "What if they locked Derol in that pantry?" His voice was solemn.

"Dang. I didn't think of that. Wouldn't he have called out or something? I mean, this is Derol. He couldn't have stayed quiet that long even if he'd tried."

Jase just looked at me, but the slanting rays of the sun were between the two of us now, and I couldn't tell if my words had made an impression on him or not.

I sighed. "I'll get the screwdriver out of the toolshed. Flat head or Philips?"

"Better get both," he said as I started toward the side of the house.

I walked away, muttering under my breath. There was no way I could let him go back alone. There was no way my Gramps was going to let me take off again, either. Especially not without telling him the reason why. I was afraid if he knew we'd been inside the old school, he might tell me I couldn't go off all over town the way Jase and I always did. He was pretty lenient with me, and I appreciated that. I didn't want to mess it up. Wonder if Billy Bob is finished with practice yet? I glanced up at the lowering sun. It seemed like it should be about time for practice to end. Sometimes it was almost dark before the coach let them go. Then it occurred to me that Billy wouldn't be practicing today. He'd said the trainer was making him sit out for a few days until his eye was better. That reminded me that Fred was the one who had hit him. Sure seeing a new side of Fred today. 'Course it wasn't actually him that frightened me at the school. It was that brother of his. I rummaged through Gramps's tools until I found both screwdrivers, before hurrying to the front of the house.

"You can't go by yourself," I said as I handed over the tools.

Jase just draped his leg over his bike and tucked the screwdrivers in his back pocket. "I have to find out if he's trapped in there," he said. "I'll give these to you tomorrow."

I put my hand on his handlebars. "If he is in there, then that means Fred and his brothers probably put him there, and they probably looped the chain through the door handles to scare us so that we wouldn't come back." He just stared off into the distance with that hard look. "They're probably still there, too." I puffed my breath out on that last syllable to let him know I was seriously worried about that possibility.

Jase finally looked at me. "What if they went back in there and Derol is trapped in that pantry? What do you think they might do?"

I shook my head. For the first time in my life, I didn't rush to help someone. And it was all because I was afraid, not so much for me, but for Jase. I knew if he went back there something awful was going to happen. "I have an idea," I said suddenly.

His eyebrows went up, but his foot was still on the pedal, ready to take off.

"What if Derol is at home already?" I looked down the street toward Karla's old house. "It's possible that it wasn't even him that we heard. You've gotta admit, that little girl can appear anywhere at any time. I just don't think Derol could've been that quiet." He appeared to be thinking about that. "Would you just check his house before you go? It's only a block out of the way." I took my hand off his handlebars and stepped back. I didn't have to tell him why I couldn't go with him. And I certainly didn't have to tell him why I didn't want him to go alone. I was sure he'd seen the fear on my face when he came up from behind of Fred and Will.

"Okay," he said at last. "If he still isn't there, I'm headed to the school to look. I'll call you later."

All my worries were for naught, because at that very moment Derol and his mom drove by. They appeared to be coming from the direction of Derol's house.

The look on Jase's face was a mixture of relief and disbelief. Without a word he took the screwdrivers from his back pocket and handed them to me. Then, with a wave of his hand, he took off.

I couldn't get the smile off my face as I walked through my own front door.

"Well, you look awful pleased about something." Gramps stood at the counter in one of Gran's old aprons. He was breading minute steaks in a mixture of egg and milk, then laying them on a plate piled high with flour. Gran's grease-filled iron skillet heated on the stove. Chicken fried steak, my favorite.

"Found Derol," I said, popping a chunk of raw potato into my mouth. "Want me to put these in the water?"

"Please," Gramps said without missing a beat. "Give the water a pinch of salt, too. Makes it boil faster."

I did as he asked. After the potatoes were boiled, I would mash them with milk and butter and Gramps would make some gravy out of the steak drippings. I could hardly wait.

"Where was he?"

Gramps's question startled me. I'm ashamed to admit I was so hungry I'd already forgotten about poor Derol. "Oh, I don't know. We just now saw him in the car with his mom. Technically, I guess she's the one who found him. Or maybe he finally went home on his own." I bit into another crisp chunk of potato. The rest were already boiling away in the pot of salted water. "I wonder where they were going." I recalled his statement about the psychiatrist.

Gramps shook his head. "The important thing is, he's safe with his mom now."

I nodded, and then I told him the details of the awful scene at lunch. He didn't say much, but I could tell he was taking it all in. He hated a bully as much as I did. I almost told him about the scene at the old school, too. I didn't want to make him worry needlessly, so I did what I always do when I don't want to talk about something. I changed the subject.

"Gramps..." I hesitated, suddenly not sure if I wanted to broach this topic with him either.

"What is it, Sprout?" He was cleaning his floury hands under the running water in the sink. The steaks were bubbling gently in the hot grease.

"There's this Halloween dance at school, and Jase wants us to go together. It's a costume dance, though." As soon as the words were out of my mouth, I knew what we had to do. That happens to me a lot. I'll worry and worry about something, and then the minute I talk about it out loud, the answer just comes to the surface like bubbles in hot grease.

"Costumes, huh?" Gramps had his back to me at the sink so I couldn't see his expression.

"Yep. And I think I just figured out who we can dress up as." I retrieved my copy of The Outsiders from my stack of books on the table.

I flipped to the part where the author described the red-haired girl known as Cherry Valance. Without thinking, I wandered back to my bedroom, imagining myself with cherry colored hair. Jase would make an excellent Ponyboy, or maybe Sodapop, the handsome one. On the other hand, he's tall like the older brother, Darry. Hmm, so many choices. I could hardly wait to tell him.

Just as I got to my bedroom, Gramps called out, "Stevie-girl? Will you set the table?" I laid the open book face down on my dresser to mark my place, then remembered how Mrs. Kennedy always scolded us for doing that, saying it would break the book's spine, so I turned back to close it properly. When I did, I was sure I saw movement in my dresser mirror. I shivered and steeled myself for the inevitable encounter with the little girl, but there was no one there. Without another thought, I grabbed my fuzzy pink robe off the hook on the back of my bedroom door and draped it haphazardly over the mirror. Then I hurried to the kitchen to set the table. Guess we weren't eating in front of the TV tonight.

After a delicious meal, Gramps and I washed dishes together, and I went off to take my bath while he settled down in the living room with the television. I heard the familiar strains of Gunsmoke on the TV, or maybe it was Bonanza. I loved them both, but sometimes I got the music mixed up.

As I made my way down the hall, listening to the western tune from the living room, my mind was way ahead of me, in the bathroom, looking into the mirror, attempting to figure out a way to NOT see the little girl again. I should be used to it by now, I thought. But no matter how many times she appeared to me—twitching and falling to the floor, eyes rolling—it was never any easier. In fact, each time she came, and I knew she was almost at the point of falling; I began to dread it even more. It had occurred to me that perhaps she was showing me her death scene. I hoped not. I hoped she hadn't died in such an awful fashion, but she was a phantom, so it was only logical to think she had died just as I saw her now. As a child. All alone.

I stopped outside my bathroom door. That's exactly what the

phantom pilot had told Jase when he first encountered him near his crashed plane: "We're all alone."

I assumed he meant we are all alone when we die. But maybe that wasn't it at all. Maybe he meant the people who became phantoms were alone when they died. Especially those who died violently or unexpectedly, the way he had. Or under mysterious circumstances the way his fiancé, Rennie Taylor, had. So maybe this little girl had died violently or mysteriously, too. I was standing in front of the mirror now, my courage revved up as high as possible, and she didn't disappoint me.

As soon as she appeared, like black smoke rising out of the bathtub reflected behind me, I started talking. Fortunately, Gramps had the western turned up as loud as our old RCA TV would go, so I was certain he couldn't hear me.

"Hello," I said. "I'm not going to run away this time. What can I do?"

Her transparent eyes locked onto mine and I could see that she was even more terrified than me. I steadied my nerves as she began to twitch. Just like Derol. She couldn't help herself. She wasn't doing it to frighten me.

Her gaze shifted toward the door as if she'd heard someone coming. I let my own gaze follow hers, and then she began to float upward until I could see her little black shoes pointed toward the floor. She fell, like always, and began to thrash violently before dissipating like a mist in front of a fan.

I realized I was holding my hand over my mouth. At least she no longer played that game of pretending to be me in the mirror. Now, she always appeared just as she was. Maybe she was beginning to trust me. "I'll help you if I can," I said softly, to no one at all. "I will stop by the library tomorrow and see if—"Then I realized I didn't have to go to the library. I turned on the bathtub faucets so the rushing water would cover the sound of my movements, and hurried into my mom's old room across the hall.

I hadn't been in this room in months. In fact, neither Gramps nor I spent much time in here. It was almost the same way she had left it so many years earlier. When my Gran was still alive, I would sometimes happen upon her in there, sitting on the bed, holding an old rag doll that she had made for my mom eons ago. The doll's name was Sarey. She had dark, curled-yarn hair and embroidered blue eyes, and I was told Mom had named it after her grandmother, Sara, my Gran's mother.

I picked up Sarey and gave her a little squeeze. She was mine, now that Gran and Mom were gone. I vowed to move her into my room tonight. Then I went to the bookshelf were Mom had kept her small collection of books and photo albums. I knew every volume on this shelf by heart. We had read most of them together, even before I was old enough to understand the words. The Little House books, Five Little Peppers, Little Women, Silver Chief, Dog of the North. But that wasn't what I was looking for. There were several slim books stacked on the bottom shelf, lying flat on top of each other.

Hurrying, because of the water running in the tub, I pulled all three volumes out and slipped them under my arm. I grabbed Sarey off the bed and rushed back to the bathroom where I opened the first book on the counter. Our High School Years was the title on the first page inside of this book. Though I was tempted to page through until I found the picture of my mom as a teen with her hair curled and her lipstick on, I knew it would have to wait until later.

I closed that one, and picked up the next volume. The name of this one was stamped in gold on the front cover. Moving Up, it read. Our Junior High Years. Nope, that wasn't the right one either. The third one was it. At the Crossroads: Our Elementary Years. Even in my hurry, I had to admire the play on words. Okay, this had to be it. In the mirror, the little phantom appeared to be about ten, maybe twelve years old at the most.

With shaking fingers, I reached over, turned off the spigots, then flipped to the fifth and sixth grade photos. Crossroads was a small town today. Back then it was barely a smudge on the map. One book listed the students for the last year my mom was there. I scanned the pictures in the fifth grade class, but I didn't see anyone who resembled the little girl.

I turned another page to check out the one and only sixth grade class, and there she was, my mom. She was just about my age, a little younger. Her hair was lighter than mine, and she wore it bobbed short with a girly headband holding it off her forehead, but those small, almond eyes could have been mine. Pain flared briefly inside me. Would I never get used to the ache of losing her? I took a deep breath and clasped Sarey tightly. Until that moment, I hadn't even realized I was still holding her.

And then I saw her, the little phantom girl. She was staring out of her own photograph just a row further down from my mother. Her wild white hair was tamed in braids, like mine, but her pale skin and eyes were exactly the same as now. She even had on a dark colored dress. I studied her delicate face. Her gaze seemed to stare across time.

Trembling with excitement, and maybe just a little bit of fear, I ran my index finger down the row of names until I got to the one that corresponded with her picture. Sally Jean Evans. "Sally Jean," I murmured, and just like that, she was back. I didn't even flinch. I looked right into her strange, pale eyes and said, "Hello, Sally Jean. Did you know my mother?"

She glanced down at the book lying open on the bathroom counter, and then she nodded. I swear she did. As before, she began to twitch and shudder, and in seconds she was swishing back and forth in front of me. I closed my eyes, briefly, when she floated upward before falling to the floor. When she had glanced away from me, toward the door, I hadn't followed her gaze. I had simply studied her instead. I was suddenly positive this elementary annual was the connection between us.

I turned another page and found a class picture in which Sally Jean and my mother were standing side by side, holding hands like best friends. I was certain I'd found the connection. Now, if I could only figure out why she was contacting me after all this time. These yearbooks had been here all along. Nothing about them had changed. So what was the catalyst? Why appear now?

I propped Sarey up on the counter, peeled off my clothes, and stepped gingerly into the tepid bath water. I wanted to add some hot water, but I'd gotten it pretty full already. To add more I'd have to let some out. So I just gritted my teeth, washed quickly, and rushed to get ready for bed. Maybe my subconscious would work on the problem while I slept, and if I talked it out with Jase tomorrow, I was sure the answer to this mystery would present itself.

14

I t wasn't until lunchtime that Jase and I caught up to Billy Bob. He was not happy. "Why so glum?" I asked around a mouthful of grilled cheese sandwich.

Billy stuffed the remainder of his first sandwich into his mouth. I'd never seen him so down. "Got benched," he said.

"Because?"

He tilted his head so I could see his still-bloodshot eye. "Coach said the trainer won't let me play until the vessels are healed."

I didn't see the problem. "That's a good thing, Bill. If you got hit again, it could do some permanent damage, right?"

He just shrugged. "It wasn't my fault, and I shouldn't be punished just for a little injury."

I was about to argue some more, try to get him to see that it wasn't punishment. It was concern for his well-being, but Jase shook his head and interrupted. "How long do they think it will be before you can play again?"

Starting on his second sandwich, Billy muttered, "A few days probably."

We all sat there in a little cloud of gloom. I knew what Jase was getting at. This coming Friday we were set to play our archrivals, the Barrett Badgers. They had gone to State last year, but we'd given them a run for their money. This year we were all set to trounce them. In band, we had the victory song down pat. Without Billy in the game, it would be very tough. He was one of the main defenders of the quarterback.

I threw some bread crusts to a shiny black grackle strutting around the tables looking for handouts. He hopped over, grabbed it, and flew a couple feet away before he began to tear it into little pieces. Soon, half a dozen appeared, seemingly, out of nowhere. "Anyone hear any rumors about Derol?" He wasn't in school, which didn't surprise any of us.

"Nah," Billy Bob said. "Fred was absent, too. Hope he isn't sick. Without him or me, the Cougars don't have a snowball's chance at Friday's game." Fred was the other guard responsible for making certain the quarterback had plenty of time to make the play.

"Ahh," I looked at Jase. "Now I see why you're so depressed."

Billy nodded. "Not a snowball's chance in Hades." He downed his milk and started on an apple without a pause.

Jase's eyes were dark. I was pretty sure we were thinking the same thing. Fred was probably skipping school today because he was afraid to come and face us. It had been very strange running into him and his brothers at the old school yesterday. I still wasn't convinced they were the ones inside the school when we were, but Jase said it was too coincidental. He didn't believe in coincidences.

Before school, I had filled Jase in on the little girl's identity.

"Sally Jean Evans." He'd said her name slowly, as if he might find some meaning there.

"Yep." I showed him the yearbook. I didn't linger over my mom's picture, though I saw him stop at it and touch her name, lightly, with his forefinger.

He'd been sitting at our kitchen table as usual. This morning we'd had scrambled eggs and bacon with biscuits. I made mine into a little sandwich, though Gramps ate his on a plate with butter and jelly. Without asking, Jase made himself a biscuit sandwich, too. For some reason that made me smile, like we were family or something.

Gramps went on to work after reminding me to come straight home after school. I blew him a kiss out the back door, and assured him I'd be there when he got home.

Jase was washing our plates in the sink when I turned back around. I wondered if he'd seen me blow the kiss to Gramps, but for some reason, it didn't worry me anymore. It seemed like we'd passed some hurdle or something at the school yesterday. Like, maybe, he'd seen me at my worst—frightened out of my wits, even more than in the old haunted Taylor house—so now everything else was just sort of normal. That felt good. As if I could finally be myself, without having to always wonder what he was thinking.

I ran to my room and got the yearbook. My robe was still draped over the dresser mirror. I'd been up before Gramps even had a chance to come in and wake me.

When I placed the book on the table, Jase knew immediately what it meant. "I can't believe we didn't think of this earlier," he said.

I couldn't believe it, either. I just never thought of my own mom being as young as the little phantom student. I guess kids never think of their parents as anything other than grownups.

"Amazing," Jase murmured, when he saw the picture of Sally Jean and my mom holding hands. He sat down on a chair to study it more closely. "You're the link," he said simply.

I was shaking my head. "I don't think it's just me, do you?" I sat on the chair near him, where I could see the book, too. "I mean, I've had that book all along. There has to be something else."

The kitchen was quiet except for the ticking of the old Regulator clock on the wall. We only had five more minutes before we needed to leave. I noticed how neatly Jase had stacked our plates and glasses in the drain board. It made me sad, because I could still picture my mom standing there washing dishes beside my Gran in her no-nonsense apron, but sad also because I couldn't picture Jase's mom doing that. In fact, I never saw her in anything except her Sunday clothes. She was always on her way to or from some place else, and if she was home when I went over, she was almost always in her bedroom or in her sewing room.

"Hey!" Jase's voice startled me back to reality.

I leaned over to look more closely. "What did you find?" I couldn't see anything except a bunch of very faint writing.

"Look." His finger was tapping what appeared to be a hand-written message.

"What's it say?" I couldn't read it without getting right under his nose. The message was written in pencil, and it was almost invisible after so many years.

"It's an inscription, you know, you sign my yearbook and I'll sign yours..."

"Of course!" Understanding dawned on me like a sunrise. "I never even thought about looking on the end pages."

He pushed the book over so we could both look at the message.

FREAK LOVER!

I said the words out loud, and then I looked up at Jase. That definitely wasn't what I expected to read in my mom's old year-book. "Is that right?"

Jase stood and took the book over to the counter and held it under the light fixture above the sink. It had the brightest bulb.

"That's what it says all right." His voice was troubled. "Why would someone—" he interrupted his own sentence. "Look at this one." He held the book down so I could read another message.

"To my best friend, Ora. Love, Sally Jean." Underneath that, someone had written, "SJ is an albino & that means FREAK!"

I felt as if someone had hit me. The message looked like it had been erased, probably by my mom, but whoever wrote it had pressed down so hard with the tip of the pencil that it was still barely legible. Now I knew why the other message was so hard to read. Mom, or someone, had tried to erase them.

I also knew what an albino was. It was someone who was born with very little melanin—the stuff that gives us color in our hair and eyes, and even in our skin. There are differing degrees, of course. Some people with albinism have absolutely no melanin, or pigment. They have to be very careful in the sunlight because they could burn severely. Sometimes their eyes look pink. I thought back to the little girl in the mirror. Her eyes were almost colorless. I'd originally thought it was because she was a ghost like Mr. Gilpin, the phantom pilot. His eyes had been silver. But apparently, Sally's eyes had always been that way.

"That's horrible," I said. "Why would someone write that just because she was different?" And then it hit me like a lightning bolt. "Because she was different," I repeated. "Like Derol is different."

Jase slowly closed the book and looked at me. There were more messages, but neither of us had the heart to read them, even knowing that the little girl had been dead for years. "You think that's the connection? You? Derol? The bullies?"

I nodded, imagining everything that Sally Jean must have endured. "What do you think happened to her?" I asked. "She was so young when she died."

The clock chimed once, for the half hour, and that was our signal to hit the road. "I don't think her death was related to her, you know, albino-ness," Jase said as we were going out the door.

"Albinism," I corrected him, without thinking. "No, I don't think so, either. Not directly, anyhow. I read about it when those brothers came out with that new album, you know, the guitar stuff."

"Edgar and Johnny Winters? They're really cool, and they burn up those guitars—"

I agreed, but then, something else occurred to me. "Hey, I wonder if her lack of skin color is why she wore that long-sleeved black dress?"

Jase just looked at me like he didn't really understand what I was saying. I'd noticed before, when I mentioned something about clothes at lunch, both he and Billy Bob seemed to zone out. Guess that's one of the things I missed most about Karla. No one to discuss fashion with. I tried to explain, anyhow. "It just looks so odd," I said. "Even for the 1940s." I closed the door behind us, and we didn't speak of her anymore as we rode to school. I didn't know about Jase, but I was anxious to see if Derol would be there.

He wasn't, of course. And after our depressing lunch with Billy Bob, I headed off to choir. I hoped Mr. Morrow wouldn't ask about Derol again. On the other hand, maybe I should tell someone what happened at the old school. As I thought about what I might say, I realized I hadn't actually seen Derol there, at all. The only person I'd seen inside the building, other than Jase, had been the little phantom girl, Sally Jean. Couldn't go around telling that story to my teachers, not even Mr. Morrow. Were we making a mountain out of a molehill as my Gran used to say? Had our imaginations gotten the best of us?

I was still pondering that question when I took my place on the risers.

Mr. Morrow never asked about Derol. He never called roll, so that wasn't an issue. (He said he knew by the way we sounded if someone was missing.) No one else mentioned him, either. It was almost as if he'd never been there at all.

English went by quickly, and as we were walking out, I was about to tell Jase my idea for our costumes when Mrs. Kennedy called me back. Jase immediately stopped to wait for me, but Mrs. K. nodded at him to go ahead so he wouldn't be late to band. "Stevie will be along in a bit," she said. "Would you tell Mr. Brown for me, please?"

Jase nodded and gave me an unreadable look, worry creasing his brow. As he turned away, I saw him shove the hair off his forehead. I gulped. Was I in trouble?

"How are you doing, Stevie?" Mrs. Kennedy asked pleasantly.

"Okay, I guess." I wanted to say great, as always, but I couldn't until I found out why I was being detained.

"Don't worry," she said, laughing. "You're not in trouble." She sat down at her desk and motioned for me to sit at the desk opposite. When I was settled, she said, "I have a favor to ask of you." I think she could see the shock on my face. Teachers, in my experience at least, never asked for favors. They told you what to do and you did it. Period.

"Umm, okay." I shifted my weight slightly, sitting up straighter than usual.

Mrs. Kennedy looked down at her desk. "I've seen you talking with Derol Pavey in the hall and at lunch. In fact, you and Jase are the only ones I've seen interact with him in a positive way."

"Well, there's Billy Bob—" I started to say, but she waved my words aside.

"Billy is usually at practice after school, so he may not be much help, and I wasn't sure if I should ask you and Jase together, although if you want to enlist his aid, that's perfectly fine with me." She stopped talking and picked up a folder.

"What is it?" I asked bluntly. "Something for Derol?" I had an idea where she was headed.

Mrs. Kennedy looked relieved. "Yes, I know he lives near you, and even though he comes to me at a different class period, you seem to like him, so I was hoping you might take this makeup work to him. I can, if you don't want to. I was just sort of hoping you would be a bridge... All my classes are reading The Outsiders this nine weeks."

"I understand." I held my hand out for the folder. "He needs to catch up, and he needs a friend." It was that simple.

She placed the folder and a copy of The Outsiders in my palm. "Tell him to answer the study questions as he reads."

"Yes, ma'am." I took the work and stood to leave.

"Thank you, Stevie." She walked me to the door and patted my shoulder as I left.

That was that. I would be going back to Karla's old house, like it or not. I tried to think positively. At least now we had a reason to go and check on Derol. Should I ask him about Fred and the schoolhouse? Was it possible that he wasn't the one who was there?

I couldn't wait to get to the band hall to tell Jase about my favor for Mrs. Kennedy. By the time I got there, Mr. Brown had everyone doing the warm-ups. Thanks to Jase telling him that I was delayed in English, no one even looked at me when I hurried in, got my instrument out of the near-empty cabinet—had a quick flashback to the locked pantry cabinet at the old school—and then slipped into my chair and right into the scales. Whew. I was glad Jase was there. I hated being the center of attention, and if he hadn't taken the message for Mrs. Kennedy, I would've had to walk into the midst of the in-progress class and explain myself.

He caught my gaze when I was settled. Did he wink? Nah, I couldn't imagine Jase ever winking at anyone. He was way too serious for that. Still, he might have. It gave me something to think about as we finished the scales and segued into our kick-stomp version of the Victory song. Mr. Brown was determined we were going to win this Friday, and he made darn sure we were ready.

When we arrived at Derol's house on our bikes, I noticed the shade across the front window was half-pulled. That window looked into the dining room. I had sat there many times after spending the night with Karla. It was nice because the dining room and living room were really just one large space. I loved being able to sit at the dining table and watch Saturday morning programming while we ate our cereal.

I cleared the cobweb memories away and looked at the half-drawn shade. Two people were sitting at the table opposite each other. They were only visible from the shoulders to the hips, sort of the middle third of their bodies. But I could tell that one of them was Derol. He had on a white tee shirt and his strong brown arms made him look like a man sitting there, drinking something from a cup. Maybe it was that cup that made him seem manly. It looked like he was drinking coffee. I only knew it was Derol because of the way his body jerked every once in awhile.

The woman across the table from him was also drinking something from a cup. She was wearing a flowered housedress, the kind my Gran always referred to as a duster because it, well, I don't know why. But it was pretty. It was also apparent that they weren't expecting company.

I looked at Jase, wondering if he could possibly be feeling the same thing I was, like I was standing there spying on them. On the other hand, it also seemed as if we might be standing in a museum somewhere, looking at a famous painting. A portrait of small town life below the shade.

Jase leaned his bike against the porch rail and waited for me to put my kickstand down. We walked up onto the porch together.

Before I even rang the bell, I heard the chairs scrape the floor as they were pushed back away from the table. I guess they'd seen us, too.

Mrs. Pavey answered the door. "Hello," she said. "May I help you?"

I held out the folder. "My name is Stevie Sanders, and this is Jason Lee. We're classmates of Derol's." I tried to peer around her into the living room to see if he was lurking there, listening, but she took up most of the space, so I continued. "Mrs. Kennedy, the English teacher, asked us to bring this by. We're all reading the same book, even though we have class at different times."

His mother smiled suspiciously, then she took the folder. "That's very kind of you. To come out of your way like this."

"Oh, it isn't out of the way at all." I hurried to explain. "I live down the block." I half-turned and pointed toward my house. "Anyhow, we kinda wanted to check on Derol, too." I lowered my eyes. I suddenly wished I hadn't started down that track.

Her flowered dress swayed a bit as she shifted her weight from one foot to the other. "He's okay—" She didn't elaborate.

Jase jumped in at last. "We were there yesterday when that kid tripped him." He debated only a second before he continued. "It was awful. We tried to help, but he took off so fast."

His mother surprised us both by laughing. "Yes, he does tend to take off when he gets upset." Her tone of voice was indulgent, as if it was really nothing to be concerned about. "It's always been that way, ever since he was a tiny little thing." She turned and spoke loudly to someone behind her, or maybe in the kitchen. "It's all right, Derol. You can come out. You've got a couple of visitors." She turned to us, stepped aside, and invited us in. "Would you two care for some hot cocoa? Derol loves his cocoa on these cool fall days."

We glanced at the table where we'd seen them sitting only a few minutes earlier. The two cups, what I thought of as coffee cups, were still sitting there, abandoned. "I don't know about Jase," I said. "But I would love some."

And just like that, we were in. After a few minutes of coaxing, Derol even joined us. His mother brought two more cups— she called them mugs—of sweet hot cocoa along with a bag of tiny marshmallows for us to float on top.

"Why don't you take your friends and show them your new room, Dee?" Mrs. Pavey suggested. "We aren't finished with it, but he was quite thrilled with his new captain's bed and matching dresser." She smiled lovingly at the son who loomed over her. "When he found out I was accepted to the nursing program at the university in Lubbock, and that we were moving to the States, I thought he would worry himself to death." She had a smooth, singsong accent that was almost identical to Derol's. "His dad should be joining us, soon. He had to stay and tie up the loose ends with the sale of our house."

She tousled Derol's black hair, and he twirled away from her and down the hall. "That's one of his tics," she said matter-of-factly. "He has to twirl in and out of doorways." She must have seen the confusion on our faces, for she hurried to explain. "You know Derol has Tourette Syndrome, right?"

Jase and I both nodded, unsure what to say.

"That means that his body does things he has little or no control over—the doctors think it's a misfiring in his brain. Anyhow, every now and then, he exhibits a new tic, you know, uncontrolled movement, like the arm and leg jerks. And the barking. Although, the medicine seems to be helping with that."

I cleared my throat. "So, he does different stuff sometimes?"

His mom laughed and put her hand on her hip. "It's something new all the time. Sometimes he loses the old tics, but sometimes he just adds them to his collection. Actually, this twirling seems to be one that comes and goes."

I took a deep breath, unsure if it would be polite to voice my opinions. "It seems like the tics get worse when he is nervous." We could hear Derol in his room. It sounded like he was straightening up, moving things around.

"Oh, yes," she replied. "You are exactly right about that, Stevie."

We were walking down the hall to Karla's old room. The walls seemed to get closer and closer together the nearer we got to her room.

Jase put his hand on my back as if to keep me from turning around and fleeing out the front door. I must've unconsciously slowed. But then we were standing in front of Karla's old bedroom and everything was new and different. The pink walls were now tan, and her tie-dyed curtains and spread had been replaced with blue and brown plaid. Whew! It didn't look like the same room at all.

Derol was standing outside his open closet door. It appeared that he had thrown an armful of clothes into the closet and was about to shut the door.

"Don't you do it," his mother said, gesturing toward the closet. "Put those clothes on hangers, not on the floor."

Derol grinned, twirled, and began to pick up the clothes and hang them up.

"Mrs. Kennedy wrote some study questions for you to answer," I said.

Derol nodded, or rather bopped, his head. "Good. I like The Outsiders. We had kids like that in Manila."

I sat on the bed and proceeded to tell him and Jase all about my idea for the Halloween costumes. "And you could go as Darry," I said in a burst of inspiration. "I mean, you're tall and dark-haired like him. And you already have the same name." I thought it was brilliant, but Derol didn't seem to share my enthusiasm.

"I don't dance," he said simply. "Did they find out who tripped me?"

It was rather an abrupt topic change, but I was glad he felt comfortable enough to mention it. "Not that I know of," I admitted. "Neither of us even saw who it was, and we were right there."

"Sneaky," Derol said, deeper into the closet as he hung up the last shirt.

"Believe me," Jase said. "If we knew who it was, we would have chased them down and hauled them to the office for you."

At that, Derol turned and looked straight at Jase as if seeing him for the first time. "For me?"

"You bet. Nothing worse than a yellow-bellied coward picking on people for no reason."

Derol seemed to consider this as he twirled his way out of the closet. "But I'm weird," he said. "People always do stuff like that to weirdoes."

My heart broke when he said that. As if he deserved to be picked on because of his Tourette's. "You are not weird!" My voice may have been a bit more strident than I intended. "The idiot who tripped you, he's the one who's weird."

Derol plopped down on the carpet in front of us. Jase and I sat on the new captain's bed, me at the head, Jase at the foot. Jase appeared to be studying a bulletin board pinned with a bunch of family pictures. It hung directly opposite the bed. One snapshot showed Derol and a man who had to be his dad—they looked eerily similar—playing basketball in a driveway somewhere. I recalled Mrs. Flint saying Derol and his mom were coming here, not only because she'd been accepted into the nursing program, but also because his dad was from somewhere in West Texas.

"I am weird," Derol repeated. "You don't have to pretend not to notice. I've been this way forever." His arm jumped and one side of his face twitched.

"You may be different, but that doesn't mean you're weird. Besides, we all have differences. Otherwise, we'd all be the same." When I'd thought those words, they sounded really logical. However when I actually said them, they sounded kind of lame. "Oh, you know what I mean." I pulled my braid around and tucked the tip of it in the corner of my mouth. "Anyhow, I've got to get home. Gramps will be there any moment, and if I'm not home, he'll get weird."

Both boys laughed when I said that, so I continued, "But Derol?"

He looked at me, and his head only jerked once.

"Were you at the old school yesterday?" I hated to come right out and ask, but I felt like it was very important that we find out if he had been in there.

He jumped up like a dark-haired jack-in-the-box, and before I knew it, he was twirling through his bedroom door and back down the hall. We were left with no option but to follow along behind.

"You two have to be going?" Mrs. Pavey sounded genuinely sorry to see us preparing to go. I guessed Derol didn't have that many visitors.

"Yes, ma'am. Don't want to get in trouble."

"No, we certainly don't want that. Thank you for coming by." She put a hand on each of our shoulders, just for a second. "You have no idea how much it means to us." She glanced at Derol for emphasis, but he was pretending to study something on the sleeve of his shirt.

Stupid me. I shouldn't have confronted him like that.

"Oh, you're welcome," I said. "Anytime Derol needs makeup work or anything, I'll be glad to get it."

"Maybe Derol could ride to school with us tomorrow," Jase piped up. "If he wants to, that is."

Everyone was quiet for a moment, remembering the day before yesterday when he'd ridden his bike for the first time.

"Could I, Nanay, I mean, Mama?" Derol glanced at us to see if we'd heard the Filipino term for mama. I guess he was trying to hide his heritage, too. He must've seen it as just one more thing that made him different. Then he asked again, surprising us all. "Could I, please?"

His mom looked at us in silence. It made me think she was weighing the risks of letting him travel that far, alone. In light of the bullying incident, that is. "We'll talk about it," she said at last. "We'll talk."

We hopped off the porch and got on our bikes. "I guess I'd better get on home, too," Jase said.

"Okay, see ya." I headed one way. He headed the other. Then something else occurred to me and I called him back.

He rode back, a question in his eyes. "What is it? Did you call me back to tell me which Outsider I should be for the dance?"

I felt my face grow hot. "We don't have to do that," I said. "It was just an idea."

Jase laughed. "I kinda like the idea, Cherry. But who will I be?"

I looked away. "You could be Sodapop, the handsome one."

He didn't say anything.

I glanced up to see if he was mad or making fun or something, but he had a big grin on his face. Whew. My stomach stopped flipping.

"But I think it's gonna be Ponyboy. He's the one who's good friends with Cherry. Soda's not."

I changed the subject. "I called you back because I remembered we were going to work for Mr. Pearcy tomorrow, but we forgot about the football game."

Jase bonked his forehead with the heel of his hand. "Think we should go over there now?"

I glanced down the block toward my house. Gramps had just pulled up in the drive. "C'mon," I said. "Let's tell Gramps. I don't think he will mind if I go today."

Gramps said it was okay, and since Jase could pretty much do whatever he wanted, whenever he wanted, away we went.

15

That night, I couldn't sleep for worrying about things. Derol had seemed pleased to see us after the shock wore off, and before I opened my big mouth about the school. He even seemed glad that Mrs. Kennedy had sent him some work. That made me wish I had asked a couple of the other teachers if they had any work for him. It also made me wonder if they had already given up on him since they hadn't bothered to send any on their own.

I got up to get a glass of chocolate milk. Sometimes that helped me get back to sleep. I still had the robe over my bedroom mirror, and the phantom student didn't scare me like she did at first, so if I did have to go to the bathroom again after drinking the milk, I thought it would be all right.

Our house was right on the corner of the street. That meant the streetlight shone down on our front yard like a full moon all the time. I quietly made my milk and settled into the sofa to drink it. Our sofa was placed directly beneath the picture window looking into the front yard. Gently, I pushed aside the curtain, recalling the scene of Derol and his mom sitting at their dining table in Karla's old house. Why had it made such an impact on me, that tableau in thirds?

I gazed out the window as I thought about it. The night was cool and cloudy, and the dirt from the just—harvested cotton fields outside town skirled in soft rills back and forth across the empty street.

A feeling of melancholy enveloped me, and I downed my milk in two gulps. I didn't want to go back to my room and stare at the ceiling, so I turned the television on low, but the only thing playing was a test pattern of bars of color on a black background. The other two channels were just snow.

I unfolded Gran's crocheted afghan from the back of the couch and curled up like a caterpillar inside a cocoon. I fell asleep to the sound of snow on TV and questions circling itself in my mind. What will I be when I awake? What will I become?

The next morning, Gramps began to move about in his room. Quickly, I got up and refolded the afghan so he wouldn't know I'd spent the night on the couch. I'm not sure why I didn't want him to know how I was feeling, but it seemed shameful somehow, to be so sad when I really had so much to be thankful for.

At Mr. Pearcy's house the day before, I had made short work of the sweeping, mopping and dusting while Jase and Mr. P. had carefully cleaned the fall leaves out of the gutters.

As I was getting dressed, I spied the book, Are You There God? It's Me Margaret, and it made me wonder if a lot of what I was experiencing could just be part of growing up. Could that really be it? I felt like two different people. Half the time I was on top of the world, and the other half I was worried to death about what people thought of me.

So what must it be like for someone like Derol? Or the little phantom? If I thought growing up was tough, what must it be like for someone who was different in a really visible way?

That gave me some perspective and I finished getting ready for school with a new outlook. Thinking about it later, I couldn't believe I'd spent the night on the couch. That was the first time I'd ever done that.

Jase ate a bowl of cereal with me and then we took off. We left a couple of minutes early to go in the opposite direction so we could stop at Derol's house. I was pretty sure his mom would let him ride with us if he really wanted to. And sure enough, when we got close, we could see him in the yard, his notebook strapped to the pumping platform behind his seat.

"Hey," I called. "Glad you're coming with us."

His mom stepped out on the porch in her student nurse's uniform. "You three go straight to school. And don't forget to lock your bikes."

"Yes, ma'am," we said in unison. Then we all laughed self-consciously. She probably didn't know that Jase and I did this all the time.

The ride to school was completely uneventful. When we got there, I caught Jase peering carefully at the lock Derol used to hook his bike chain to the rack. It was the same brand as the one we'd seen before. All of a sudden, I was dying to go back to the old school and see if the other shiny lock had been placed back on the chain there.

As usual, while he was in motion, riding his bike, Derol's tics were almost nonexistent. However, the moment we stopped and got off to lock the bikes to the rack, his arm flopped up and his head jerked to one side. Then he twirled through the doorway ahead of us amidst the stares of a dozen other kids.

The day went fairly smooth. Everyone was focused on the game against the Badgers that night. Billy Bob was sour and silent at lunch. He was still benched, but his eye appeared to be back to normal to me. He didn't want to talk about it, though, so we didn't. He did say he thought Coach was going to let Fred play even though he had missed practice the day before. That was usually an automatic benching for the next game, but since he was out, Billy thought Coach might keep Fred in.

"Who knows?" I said naively. "Maybe he'll bench Fred and let you play instead."

Both Jase and Billy looked at me like I'd lost my mind. Apparently, I just did not grasp the intricacies of team sports. Fortunately, Derol arrived at that moment, safely I might add, and we all began to talk about where to sit at the game. Jase and I were in the band so, of course, we had to sit there, but Derol could sit in the student section for free if he went.

He shook his head when we mentioned it. "No, no. I won't be there."

I wanted to ask why, but I knew the answer. Who would he sit with? Most likely, his mom wouldn't even let him go, unless she decided to go with him or something.

We made it through the rest of the day without any major incidents. I think having Derol back in choir made everyone happy, especially him.

After school, I went straight home, ate a sandwich with Gramps, and changed into my band uniform. After we picked up Jase, Gramps took us to the football field. I was glad the game was in Crossroads and not in Barrett. I liked riding the bus, but if we were going to have any chance at beating them, it would have to be on our own turf. Though to be honest, I didn't have the grudge against them that Billy did. To me, it was just another chance to march and sit out in the sweet night air watching the June bugs swarm the stadium lights. I guess I'm sort of simple, because that's the way I like to spend my time. Of course, it didn't hurt that Jase would be there, too.

In between playing the songs in the stands, marching at half-time, and being part of the unofficial pep squad when we weren't playing, I guess I wasn't really watching the game. All of a sudden, the visitor side of the stadium erupted in cheers and my eyes immediately went to the scoreboard. Nothing had changed. The game was still tied 7—7 and we had the ball. So why were they cheering?

And then I saw it. Our quarterback had been sacked and now Barrett had the ball and was headed for the end zone. Oh, dear. I pulled my clarinet up, because I figured Mr. Brown would signal us to play the "Push 'Em Back" song, but we never got that far. Instead, Barrett made the touchdown, and they made it look easy. They kicked the extra point and our guys came to the sidelines in a cloud of misery that was almost palpable.

Coach had allowed Fred Green to play after all and when he walked by Billy Bob, who was furiously warming the bench, he said something that appeared to start with the letter F.

Billy Bob came off the bench, threw his helmet down, and bowed up at Fred like a rooster at a snake. Fred turned and said something else, and Billy tackled him and took him to the ground right there in front of Coach and everybody.

Sandy Morrison was there in an instant. Even from this distance, I could hear him shouting at Fred, "If it wasn't for you, he wouldn't be riding the bench." Then Coach was there, too, in between them, pointing and demanding both boys go with the assistant coach to the locker room to cool off.

I wasn't exactly sure what Fred had said, but it must have been bad. I'd never seen Billy jump on anyone like that. It was weird and frightening. As if someone else had control of him.

It certainly didn't help the game, either. The fight seemed to have gone out of all the boys after that, and although the final score was close, the Badgers still won.

After it was over, I found Gramps in the parking lot and we stood for a moment while Jase loaded his bass drum on the band truck. His parents hadn't been able to attend the game.

Sometimes, if they had other things to do, we would drop him off at home.

As we stood beside the truck, Gramps visiting with Bobby Tucker's dad, Billy came walking by with his family. His dad had one arm draped casually over his son's shoulders as if he was afraid of what might happen if he turned him loose.

Jase appeared about that time and he and Billy stopped, toe-to-toe. Billy shook his head morosely, looking at the ground and muttering something before he walked on to the family station wagon.

"What'd he say?" I asked Jase when he got into the truck with us.

For a second or two, I didn't think he was going to tell me. Then he said, "He told me this all would have been avoided if he hadn't stood up for Derol that day the guys were making fun of him in the field house."

I looked at my reflection in the curve of the night-black windshield. It shouldn't be so difficult to do the right thing, should it? I thought back to the pictures of Vietnamese people lying in torn heaps on the ground. This is nothing, I wanted to say. Of course, I couldn't say that at all, not with Gramps sitting in the driver's seat. He thought he'd hidden that paper. Besides, I wasn't the one with a black eye and no game. Who was I to say what was right and what was wrong? All I could do was follow my own heart. Most of the time, that was difficult enough.

The ride home was nearly silent except for Merle Haggard on the old truck's radio. When we let Jase out at his house, I saw Gramps's mouth go tight. "You sure somebody's home, son?"

"Yes, sir," Jase replied. "I can see the glow of the TV through the curtains there."

"All righty then, give my best to your folks."

Jase said he would, and then he thanked us for the ride and started toward the door. From the fence line, I heard Buddy whicker. Jase waved at us and then changed course, heading for the corral.

It had been a while since I'd had a chance to visit Buddy. "Would it be okay if I ride out tomorrow to ride Buddy?"

Gramps nodded, looking both ways before pulling out of the drive. Jase's folks never shut the big iron gate unless they were going to be gone out of town or something. "If you will tell me what that fight was about during the game."

I couldn't believe it. My own grandpa was blackmailing me. I grinned. On second thought, he was an ex-cop. He'd stop at nothing to get information if he wanted it. "Well, you heard what Billy Bob told Jase, right?"

"I did..."

I took a deep breath, unsure how to begin. "I know you haven't met Derol Pavey yet, but he's different. He's from the Philippines and he's got this thing called Tourette Syndrome." I stopped to breathe, trying to think of the best way to describe it.

"Yep, I knew another boy who had that. Back before your time. We called him Chicken Little because he made squawking noises all the time."

I was stunned into silence. My own Gramps, the man who could do no wrong, used to make fun of a boy with Tourette's?

"Close your mouth, Stevie-girl. You might catch a fly. I was a kid once, too. Been awhile, though. And back then, we didn't know he couldn't help himself. We thought he liked making everyone laugh." He clicked on the turn signal for our street. "We just thought of him as our class clown."

"What became of him?" I asked. I wanted to ask how the boy felt about being known as the class clown just because he had something he couldn't do anything about, but I didn't want to sound like a goody-two-shoes. If I'd lived way back then, I might've called him names just like the other kids.

We pulled into the carport and Gramps got out of the truck

before he answered. "He became the mayor of Crossroads, Texas," he said. Then he turned and waltzed in the house, pretty as you please, leaving me standing on the porch catching flies.

"But, Gramps," I called as I followed him inside. "How did he get rid of his tics, and his squawking?" Crossroads was a very small town. Everyone knew Mayor Stone.

Gramps was standing in the kitchen, looking in the refrigerator. He held up the gallon of milk questioningly. I nodded and went to take down the glasses and the Nestle's Quik.

"I asked him that myself one day, over at the café," he said.

We sat at the table where I stirred my milk. Gramps brought a bag of Pecan Sandies to the table and we each took one.

"Well?" I was impatient. If the mayor could overcome it, surely Derol could, too. I couldn't wait until Monday so I could tell him this story.

Gramps leaned back in his chair. "We gave him a real hard time there for awhile," he admitted. "I think we were about your age. It got so bad his Daddy took him plumb outta school and drove him to Dallas to find out what was making him jerk and flail about so."

We each dunked a cookie and munched silently. I took a big gulp of milk and wiped at my mouth with the back of my hand, completely forgetting my manners in my quest to find out more. "When did he come back? Is Dallas where they found he had Tourette's? When did you—"

Laughing, chugging down his own milk, Gramps continued. "I didn't see him again until I came back from the war in the mid-forties. By then, he was already married to Betty Shaffer. They had a couple of little girls, and he was working for the city in the accounting department."

"But did they cure him somehow? He doesn't jerk or bark or anything like Derol does." I was still trying to reconcile an image of Derol twirling through doorways with the image of Mayor

Stone riding in the parade in that big red convertible Cadillac every Fourth of July.

"I couldn't believe it myself," he said. "So I asked him what they'd done to him while he'd been away. He said he got some medicine and some therapy that helped him control some of his outbursts. And he said he just got older, that sometimes growing up can cure some of the tics, especially the ones that get worse around other people. I think getting away from us kids helped him, too. His parents had some money, thank goodness. They put him in a special school up there, with some other kids that had problems fitting in—"

"Like Sally Jean Evans? Mom's best friend?" I don't know why I didn't think to ask him about her earlier. He would've known Sally. He was my mama's daddy, after all. I guess there had simply been too much going on for me to be able to think straight.

Gramps's hand stopped halfway to his mouth with a second cookie. "Sally Jean?" He gave me a searching look. "What made you think of her?"

Oops. Think fast. "Oh, I was reading Mom's old yearbooks— not a lie, not even a fib—and I saw where she'd written a note to Mama. Said they were best friends."

He set the remainder of his cookie on the table as if it had lost its flavor. "How'd you know she didn't fit in?"

Now my cookie tasted bad. "There were some awful things written there by other people." I took my glass to the sink. "They called her an albino freak." I winced as I recalled those words pressed into the endpapers of the yearbook so hard they felt like inside-out Braille. "I closed it after I read that. I didn't want to see any more."

Gramps just sat quietly. I almost wished I hadn't brought it up. His shoulders were sort of hunched, and he looked a lot older than he had when we sat down a few minutes earlier. "She was your Mama's best friend. Your mom fought a few battles over Sally Jean."

I stood very still, my back to him. In the reflection of the dark kitchen window, I could see Sally Jean standing behind him at the table. I'd never seen her outside the mirror before, except in the schoolhouse. I closed my eyes when she reached toward him, afraid she would shudder and fall. I didn't want to see what would happen if she actually touched him, either.

When I opened my eyes, Gramps was rubbing his hand across the back of his neck as if he'd caught a chill. Sally was nowhere to be seen.

16

"She was picked on even worse than we picked on Donnie Stone back in my day." He brought me his glass. I rinsed it out and set it in the drainer.

"Did she come home with Mama a lot?" I tried to sound casual. I didn't want him to think I was too interested.

"She spent some time here, that's for sure." His mild blue eyes were dreamy. I could see his reflection just as I'd seen hers a moment earlier. "I think your Mama was her only friend."

I felt a warm tear slip out. I didn't even know it was there. "What happened to her?" I was half-afraid he wouldn't tell me. That it would be too awful and he would try to hide it the way he'd tried to hide the article about the My Lai massacre.

But he did tell. "There was a dance at school. It was a fall dance, and they didn't let them wear costumes that year for some reason." He lumbered back to the table and sat down. "She walked over with your Mama. They were just going to stay long enough to bob for apples, have some punch, and come home. Sally didn't really want to go—I remember that. But your mom wanted to, so they decided to compromise and only go for a little while."

I sat down across from him. "Then what?"

He ran his hands around the edge of the old Formica table. He was obviously remembering as he went. "They wound up staying for two hours. Your mama called me from the office and told me they were staying later. They were having so much fun bobbing, playing games, dancing. No one messed with Sally when your mom was around."

His hands were rubbing holes in the Formica. He wasn't here at all. He was firmly back there, on that night. "I should have driven over and picked them up, but I didn't. They walked down Sixth Street from the school. It was their last year before junior high. When they got to the corner, Sally turned off on Avenue J to go to her house, and your mom came on inside." His hands had stopped. They gripped the edges of the table tightly.

I caught a glimpse of movement. Was Sally listening from the hallway?

"Sally's mother showed up shortly after your mom went to bed. Mrs. Evans was frantic because Sally hadn't come home. I immediately called Chief Galloway, and he came over with a couple other officers."

"What did they say?" I leaned forward. The tabletop was cold beneath my forearms. I was pretty sure Sally Jean was nearby. The temperature always dropped a few degrees when she was around.

"They wanted to know if she had stayed here with your mom." He was talking faster now, as if he would get it all out and be done with it. "Gran got her out of bed and we all sat right there, in the living room." He jerked his thumb over his shoulder, indicating where they had sat. "'Course your mom had to tell them everything that happened. How she'd last seen Sally when they split off at the corner." He was silent for a moment. I was afraid that he was finished.

"Did they leave then? Did they go find her?" My heart was a

stone in my chest. Now, my hands were gripping the table. What was that sound? The flesh on my arms crinkled. Cold again.

"Together, we searched the neighborhood for hours. Even brought in Red Arley's old bloodhound to see if he could pick up her scent."

"And did he? Pick up her scent, I mean?" I could feel my pulse quickening as he neared the end of his story.

"He did," he said. "Tracked her right back to the school. 'Course everyone thought he'd just followed her scent from where her and your mama first went to the dance. They weren't even gonna search it, but your mom insisted. She told them how the kids, especially a certain group of boys, always teased Sally and called her names."

Albino freak flashed into my mind.

"They asked her if any of those boys had been at the dance, and your mama started naming names. The Cole boys, Tank Green, a couple of other kids whose names I've forgotten. She said they didn't mess with Sally at the dance, though. They wouldn't dare when she was around." Gramps chuckled a bit. "Your mama didn't take no sh—stuff off anyone."

Tank Green? That name leapt out at me like an alley cat from a trashcan. Something fell to the floor in my room. I jumped and looked at Gramps in surprise. We hurried down the hall.

Sarey lay on the floor, but it wasn't the old rag doll that had made the noise. She was just an embroidered bag of stuffing. It was Mama's old yearbook that had made the loud thunk. It lay on the floor beside Sarey. And it was open to the page where the ugly inscriptions were written.

Gramps walked over and picked up Sarey and the book. "Maybe your mama," was all he said. But I didn't think so.

I surreptitiously pulled the robe off the mirror behind Gramps's back and there was Sally, still as a doorstop, looking out. I nodded at her, and she faded away. For once, she didn't twitch and fall to the floor. Maybe I was finally getting through to her. Or maybe it was because Gramps was telling her story...

Gramps closed the yearbook as if he were closing a chapter of his own life. In a way, I suppose he was. He placed it on my bedside table and laid Sarey on my pillow. Then he followed me back to the kitchen. "Now, tell me what happened to cause Billy Bob and Fred Green to get in a fight at the game."

The tone of his voice brooked no argument. I had to tell him.

Gramps's face was solemn. I always knew when his policeman's brain was taking over. His face got like this and his hands clenched up into fists until his knuckles got white. "Hit him right in the eye with his elbow, huh?"

I nodded. The shadows in the kitchen were deep. We only had the one light on over the sink. I got up to turn on the fixture over the table.

"You think the Green boy is picking on your friend Derol, too? Physically, I mean?"

I scrolled through the scant scenes of bullying in my mind. All I could say for certain was that there had been ugly remarks, and someone had tripped him at lunch. I couldn't say for sure if Fred Green was involved or not. As for the old schoolhouse, that wasn't certain either.

"I'm not sure," I admitted. "But it's strange that his last name is the same as one of the boys who teased Sally Jean." I hoped to gently steer the conversation back to what happened to her. I hated to press Gramps too much. He might clam up like he did about the My Lai article in the paper.

Gramps snorted and stood. He stretched and yawned. "Not too much of a coincidence there, Stevie-girl. Tank is Fred's daddy." He clucked loudly and shook his head. "Guess that apple didn't roll far from its seed."

My mind whirled. Another connection. An awful connection. I had to tell Jase—see what he thought about it. But it was too late to call. His mom and dad would probably be in bed and I couldn't even imagine waking them unless it was a life and death emergency—and maybe not even then. His parents were not the easiest folks to relate to. I sighed and went to get ready for bed. It would just have to wait until tomorrow.

I bathed and brushed my teeth hurriedly. Sally was nowhere to be seen.

"Night, Stevie," Gramps called from down the hall.

I heard the springs creak when he climbed into bed. It was a comfortable sound. "Night, Gramps," I called back. Then I turned out the light and climbed into my own cozy bed with Sarey. The moonlight fell softly through my open curtains. It lay across my quilt like an added layer of warmth. Unlike some people, I felt very comfortable in the night. I knew the light from the moon was really just reflected from the hidden sun, and that warmed me somehow.

I remembered the night Mom and I had driven here, to Crossroads from Dallas, after my dad took off and left us penniless. The moon had followed our car like a guardian angel all the way. When we arrived, it was two a.m. and Gramps had come out and carried me in from the car. He tucked me into this bed, under this very quilt, and I had drifted off to sleep with the very same moon sending her comforting rays through the gap in these very same curtains. If I tried, I could even conjure up the spearmint smell of the snuff can Gramps had kept lodged securely in the breast pocket of his uniform shirt.

Just before sleep carried me away, I thought I saw Sally Jean sit on the edge of my bed, but I was too far into the twilight to turn back. I just smiled and believed my sleepy brain when it told me she was only a dream.

THE NEXT MORNING dawned cold and overcast. Gramps had to work for another dispatcher who was out with pneumonia.

"You call and let me know when you get to Jase's house," he'd written on the note stuck to the fridge. He'd stuck it under the magnet I'd gotten at Six Flags the summer my daddy had taken us there. I often thought about throwing that magnet in the trash, but not because it was ugly or anything. It was a little metal magnet that showed the park with all the flags flying above it. I liked the magnet, and I'd loved the beautiful new park itself, but I'd been too small to ride most things. And Daddy got mad a time or two when I couldn't measure up to the "You Must Be This Tall To Ride" signs even when I was standing on my tiptoes. He cussed out one of the attendants and we were asked to leave. Mama was so upset. She asked Daddy why he always thought he deserved special treatment. I don't remember what he said, but it was something about how rules were made to be broken and besides, it wasn't special treatment for him—it was for me.

I fingered the little magnet now. I had never wanted special treatment. Especially not on some roller coaster that might throw me out if I didn't fit under the seat belt properly. Would Gramps notice if it went missing? What would I tell him if I threw it away and then he asked about it? I finally just left it where it was and opened the door for the milk.

After eating my cereal in front of the TV, I rinsed my bowl, had a slurp of orange juice from the pitcher in the fridge, and then I went in search of my favorite jeans and sweatshirt.

When I opened the closet door, I caught a sense of movement behind me. I turned, expecting Sally to be peering out of my dresser mirror. I'd pulled the robe off of it the night before, but she wasn't there.

She was standing right behind me instead.

I had to bite my lip to keep from yelling. This was the closest

I'd ever been to her without benefit of a mirror or a pane of glass. "How did you get out of the mirror?" I asked without thinking. I recalled how she'd been right behind Gramps last night, too. How she'd caused the book and Sarey to fall to the floor. In fact, she'd gotten braver and braver ever since I'd found the yearbook.

She still wouldn't, or couldn't, speak. She just stood there for a moment, her colorless gaze boring into mine.

"It's okay," I said, pretending to be calm. "I'll help if you tell me what to do."

Her eyes started to roll up. Her shoulders began to shake. I knew what was coming. I put my hand over my eyes.

She disappeared.

"Sally Jean?" My voice sounded funny even to me, calling a dead girl in the middle of an empty room. She hadn't shown me the death scene. Maybe when I put my hand over my eyes it made her realize how awful it was, how it affected me.

I recalled how Jase and Billy and I had cut out bold, black newspaper headlines in order to communicate with the phantom pilot last year. Should we try that again? I hurried to get dressed. Would she come with me to Jase's house? Or was she tied to one place? No, I'd seen her at the school and here at my own house. Jase had said I was her connection like his dog Lady had been the pilot's connection.

She had been my mom's best friend. Maybe she could go wherever I went.

I finished dressing, grabbed my coat from the hall closet, and away I went. Jase should be up by now. Should I go by Derol's house?

DEROL WAS in his pajamas in front of the TV. It appeared that he'd eaten a bowl of cereal there, too. Once again, I was standing on the doorstep waiting on someone to answer my knock. I'd written Karla a long letter describing everything that was going on, but I hadn't heard anything back. I began to think she didn't believe me about the phantoms. Her letters were growing shorter and further apart. In hers, she often talked about going out to movies with a whole group of friends. She went on and on about her new boyfriend. His name was Charlie, and he didn't even go to her school. She said he was an excellent kisser.

"Well, Stevie. How nice of you to drop by." Derol's mom had her nurse's uniform on, but I couldn't tell if she was about to leave, or just getting home.

"I probably should have called," I said, "but I didn't know the number." I mentally cringed when I heard how stupid that sounded, but it was only the truth. "I'm on my way out to Jase's house to visit his horse, Buddy." Talk about sounding stupid. "Anyhow," I charged ahead. "I thought Derol might want to go meet him. The horse."

Mrs. Pavey laughed good-naturedly. "Derol! Stevie's here." She stepped aside. "C'mon in and sit down. He just went to throw some clothes on."

I sat on the sofa. Derol was watching the same TV channel where I'd been watching The Monkees only moments earlier. That made me smile.

"Hi." His voice belied his confusion. "Umm, everything okay?" He was looking at my hands to see if I was carrying anything. Forgotten work, perhaps.

My smile turned to a grin. "Just came by to see if you wanted to go out to Jase's house with me. To ride his horse, Buddy."

Derol debated about two seconds, then he grabbed his coat and headed for the door. He twirled through it just as his mom said, "Hey there, son. Didn't you forget something?" Her lovely accent made everything she said sound like a gentle request to my ears, but it brought Derol up as short as a dog on a rope.

"Can I?" He danced from one foot to the other on the front porch. "Is it o-okay?"

He stuttered a bit, and I wondered if he was auditioning a new tic.

His mom looked at me sternly. "Straight there and straight home?"

I nodded. "Yes, ma'am. We can call you when we get there, if you want. That's what I do. With my Gramps, I mean."

She looked at me, and then she looked at Derol hopping around on the front porch. "I have to go to work. Doing my clinicals at the old folks home, you know."

She wrote down the number on a scrap of paper. "Call me here." She thrust the paper at me. "If they say I'm busy, just leave me a message so I'll know everything's all right."

"You bet," I said. Before I could get off the porch, Derol was unlocking his bike and heading down the drive. I noticed he'd thrown his lock and chain on the ground beside the porch rail. Heck, at home, I didn't even lock mine.

Mrs. Pavey waved from the porch as we rode away. "Don't forget to call," she said.

Derol turned around and waved once, and then we were passing my house, headed toward the old school. We had to pass Central Elementary and the hospital to reach Jase's house.

As we neared the old school, Derol began to speed up again. By the time I got near, he was getting ready to turn the corner. "Wait up," I called. "You don't even know where Jase lives!"

He didn't slow until he was far enough away that I could no longer see the big windows shadowed by the overhanging archway. Then he stopped. As soon as he stopped, his left arm flailed up and his head jerked. Should I tell him about the mayor?

"Hey," I said breathlessly. "What's the rush?"

He glanced back at the school.

"Were you in there the other day? The day that kid tripped

you at school?" I hoped I wasn't about to freak him out again, asking this, but just being near the school clearly upset him.

Derol fastened his deep black gaze on my face and nodded once. His arm flailed and his knee jerked and he started pedaling again. "I used to g-go there," he said as if it were no big deal.

"But you don't anymore?"

He shook his head. We weren't riding very fast, thank goodness.

"Something l-lives there," he said.

You could have knocked me off that bike with the suggestion of a feather. "What did you see?" I asked.

For a moment, I thought he wasn't going to answer, and then he said, "I heard something. Something b-breathing. And s-someone wrote help me in the dust."

I tried to interpret what he had said. He'd heard the breathing and he'd seen the message in the dust, so that proved he'd been in there that day. But if he wasn't the one doing the heavy breathing inside that pantry...who was?

17

All the way to Jase's house, I turned the problem over in my mind. Who was in that pantry? Who wrote in the dust? We'd thought it was Derol. But if it wasn't him, could it be that Sally Jean was the dust-writer? If so, that would be a way to communicate. If not, that really worried me. I couldn't sort it out now, so I changed the subject.

"Derol," I said, as we neared Jase's house. "What would you say if I told you I know someone else with Tourette's?"

He stopped his bike, planted his big feet on the ground and said, "Who?"

I couldn't help myself, I grinned. It was as if I had told him where the candles were when the lights went out. "Our mayor. My Gramps said he had Tourette's when they were boys in school together. But now, you can't even tell it."

Derol looked at me in disgust. I wasn't sure if it was part of his Tourette's or not, but he really had a hard time hiding his emotions. Everything he felt showed up on his face like a tattoo. "I thought you meant another k-kid." He started pedaling again. He didn't wait up.

I'll admit, that sort of burst my bubble and hurt my feelings.

I'd been so certain he would be thrilled knowing that the leader of our whole town also had Tourette's. But after giving it some thought, I decided I'd just sprung the news on him in the wrong way. I should have told him it was an adult to begin with. Instead, I'd gotten his hopes up, made him think he had a kindred spirit that he didn't know about.

"Wow." Derol stopped suddenly. He'd just spied Buddy, the palomino, standing with his head facing the wind. The breeze was blowing his taffy colored mane, and he looked just like the horse named Phantom from the book Misty of Chincoteague. Except that horse was a mare. Buddy was a gelding.

"Beautiful, isn't he?" I asked.

Derol rode slowly closer.

"Do you like to ride horses?" I asked, getting off my bike and putting the kickstand down. Jase must have seen us coming up the long drive, because he was on the porch before we'd even parked. Derol hadn't taken his eyes off Buddy.

"I never have," he said.

I waved at Jase. "Think we can ride today?" That was the good thing about Jase, and Billy Bob, too. We never bothered to ask about getting together. We just did it.

"Why not?" Jase was smiling crookedly. He was obviously enjoying the way Derol was looking at Buddy. It's always nice when someone appreciates the same things you do. I knew that first hand.

"We both have to call our folks and let 'em know we're here." I handed Derol the slip of paper his mom had given me, and we followed Jase into the kitchen to make our calls. Seeing the old sprung screen door—Lady's self-made doggie door—made my throat constrict. She had been such a good dog, even if she was a ghost.

"My tio had a horse. He lived outside M-Manila. It was a sstallion though. Too much for me. My tio rode him in p-p-parades. He did roping tricks off him."

Jase laughed. "Well, I don't know any roping tricks, but old Buddy loves for us to ride him, as long as we brush him before and after. He's kind of spoiled that way." He reached in the fridge and produced a couple of large carrots. "No one's here but us. Let's go get acquainted."

The day was perfect for riding. I loved that horse almost as much as Jase did. We all went to the barn for the tack. Derol couldn't believe how Buddy followed along behind us like a big old pet. Give that horse a carrot and he was your buddy for life. Jase said that was how he came up with the name.

In the barn, I couldn't help but remember how we'd talked to the phantom pilot out here, using our cut out letters. He had caused quite a storm in the barn, swirling things around, throwing gardening tools. I glanced out the wide-open doors, recalling the jelly goo that had fallen from the sky like sticky rain.

The little phantom girl, Sally Jean, did none of those things. I wondered if it was because she was a kid and didn't have the same power as an adult phantom, or whether it was just because she was a gentler soul to begin with. I was learning that all spirits were not created equal.

"I-I haven't really ridden a horse before," Derol said as he fed Buddy the last carrot.

Jase handed him the soft brush. "Then you'd better get on his good side first." He grinned. I liked the way he teased Derol. Everyone else was so serious around him, as if he wasn't a real boy just because he had Tourette's. He's sort of like Pinocchio.

Derol took the brush and ran it down Buddy's smooth vanilla-colored coat. Buddy turned his head to see who belonged to these new hands, and that surprised Derol so that his arm flew out to the side, and the brush went flying across the barn. Jase and I both laughed.

"It's okay," I said, retrieving the brush. "He's only looking to see who you are. He's just curious."

Taking a deep breath, Derol started brushing again. I was afraid our laughing would hurt his feelings, but I guess he realized it wasn't that kind of laughter. We were simply amused at the way Buddy rolled his big old horsey eye around to see what was going on.

"Okay." Jase took the brush from Derol and slid the brightly striped wool saddle pad on Buddy's back. Derol stepped aside, his knee jerking spasmodically.

Jase heaved the western saddle into place, tightened the cinch, and then he stepped up into the stirrup and slung his long leg over Buddy's back. Buddy trotted out of the barn into the paddock. Jase made a couple of rounds inside the fence line, warming Buddy up, and checking the saddle to make sure it was secure. We didn't usually use one, just rode bareback, but since it was Derol's first time, I guess Jase thought it would be safer with something to hold onto. Then he rode back to us and slipped off.

"Ready?" he asked Derol.

Derol's arm was flailing and his knee was jerking. "Aren't you next, S-Stevie?" His head jerked a bit when he looked at me.

"Sure." I boosted myself into the saddle, and Buddy started off before I was even settled. He loved attention of any kind.

We walked, trotted, and even galloped a little, showing off a bit for Derol. Really, it wasn't me. I simply let Buddy do what he wanted. Jase and Derol were standing outside the barn door. It looked as if they were actually conversing. I slowed Buddy and walked him back toward them just as Billy Bob rode up on his bike.

"Hey, Bill," I said in greeting.

He raised his hand to me, but his other hand was already reaching to stroke Buddy's nose. Another fan.

"Your turn," I said, handing the reins to Derol. "Just hold them like this." I demonstrated how to hold them evenly, with light pressure on the bit. "You don't want to pull back too hard or pull to one side too much. He has a very soft mouth."

Derol's left arm couldn't be still, but he took the reins in his other hand and pulled himself into the saddle using the saddle horn. Once he was up, Jase took hold of Buddy's lead rope, which he'd attached to his bridle in addition to the reins, and led him around the corral. "Just relax and get the feel of him," Jase said. "And let him get the feel of you. I'll lead him around awhile, if you don't mind."

"Good," Derol replied. He kept both hands on the saddle horn, the reins clasped loosely between his fingers. I saw him shifting his body slightly, in rhythm with Buddy's natural rolling gait, and it reminded me of the way he swayed back and forth during music class. His arms and legs were still, and even his head had stopped jerking. It was as if he were concentrating so intently on the rhythm of the ride, that his brain finally had some place to direct all that excess electricity or something. I thought about how little was known about his syndrome in our tiny school, and it made me think that perhaps it would be something I could do when I grew up. I loved researching things anyway—why not medical research? I'd recently learned, from my social studies book, that Filipino people not only spoke Spanish, they also spoke something called Tagalog. I wondered if Nanay, the word Derol had called his mom, was Tagalog.

Billy was standing with one foot on the bottom rail of the fence when the little phantom girl appeared. She was watching Derol and Buddy from the other side of the corral. I was just wondering if anyone could see her besides me, when all of a sudden, Buddy snorted and reared up on his hind legs, tumbling Derol to the ground.

"What tha..." Billy said in awe. "Never seen him do that before." He was running toward Derol as he spoke, the stem of hay he'd been chewing flying back over his shoulder as he spat it out to run.

I guess that's my answer, I thought, as I ran after Buddy. I could see that Jase and Billy were getting Derol up off the ground and dusting him off, but Buddy was headed for the open corral gate. He was getting as far away from Sally Jean as he possibly could.

Slowing to a walk, I held out my hand. I was holding the brush that Buddy loved. I had grabbed it off the hook beside the barn door thinking it might let him know everything was all right. I didn't have a carrot or anything to soothe him, or lure him. But he was having none of it. Before I got close, he bolted out the gate and headed for the backfield at a trot. He wasn't terrified—he would've been galloping if that were the case—he just seemed frightened and confused. Animals have a sixth sense, but I'm not sure they always understand what it's telling them.

"Is he all right?" I called to Jase.

Derol waved at me, a big grin on his face. "I got thrown," he said. His voice was chipper, as if falling off a rearing horse was the best thing that had ever happened to him. "Jase says I must get right back on," he called.

I laughed. "I've gotta catch him first." I was so glad he wasn't hurt or frightened, but I wasn't at all certain I could get Buddy to come back to the corral. He'd been the same way when the phantom pilot had caused the sticky goo to fall that day.

In a moment, Jase appeared beside me. "Thank goodness, he wasn't hurt. Did you see her?"

I nodded. "Do you think anyone else did, besides Buddy, I mean?"

Jase shook his head. "No, Billy was going on about how Buddy had never done anything like that before. Guess he didn't see her. I was afraid he was going to give Derol a complex, make him think it was his fault or something, so I just said it was probably the cool weather making him want to kick up his heels or something."

I laughed. "You could always say he just had a burr under his saddle blanket."

Jase grinned and clicked his tongue at Buddy. The beautiful gelding was standing at the fence, contentedly munching a long stalk of prairie grass growing through from the other side.

"I guess we need to tell Billy about Sally Jean. You gonna let Derol try to ride again?" I took hold of the loose reins while Jase ran his hands up and down the horse's neck, soothing him and telling him everything was okay. Actually, Buddy didn't look the least bit concerned now. Jase picked up the lead rope and we turned back toward the corral.

"I think he needs to," he replied. "As long as Sally isn't still around. Someone could get hurt if she does that awful twitchy thing. That scares me. It would probably send Buddy right into orbit."

"Speaking of that..."

Jase glanced up. "Yeah?"

"Do you think Sally had Tourette's or epilepsy or something? The way she twitches."

We stopped so Jase could pack dirt into a new gopher hole with the side of his shoe. Gophers were the most dangerous things for horses and riders. Many a horse had injured both themselves and their riders by stepping in those hard-to-see holes. "I don't know," he said. "Wouldn't your Gramps know if she had, I mean, it seems like she spent quite a bit of time with your mom."

"Oh! I didn't tell you. Gramps told me about the night she disappeared." I relayed the conversation to him, ending with how she had made the book and doll fall to the floor. I also told him my theory about Sally getting braver and braver. "First, she pretended to be me looking out of my own mirror. Then she appeared as herself in the mirror, then we saw her in the school, and now she seems able to materialize any place she wants."

"As long as you're nearby," Jase added. "But man, Tank Green? Fred's dad?" His voice held a note of disbelief. "What a coincidence." His hand strayed to Buddy's mane. "You know I don't really—"

"—believe in coincidences, I know." We walked along in silence for a few steps.

"So they never found her? Ever?" He pushed his own fore-lock off his forehead, and for the first time, I noticed he and Buddy had the same shade of hair.

Now it was my turn to shrug. "I'm not sure. That's when Sally knocked the stuff off in my room, and Gramps and I both ran in there. After that, Gramps didn't say anymore." I slapped the long reins gently against my blue-jeaned leg as we walked. "Maybe it's time I visited the library. Don't they keep old newspapers in the basement? I know it happened around Halloween when they were in sixth grade." My eyes sought Jase's as I realized what that meant. It was their fall dance the night Sally Jean disappeared. We were getting ready for our own fall—Halloween—dance. Another coincidence? Jase didn't seem to notice. He was thinking of something else.

"The library's a good idea. I want to go with you, though. If it really was the last time anyone saw her, that should have been a big story in the paper."

I agreed, and then I quickly told him about the fall dance

coincidence. He grimaced. I went on to tell him about Mayor Stone while I was thinking of it. He couldn't believe that, either.

"So, there's hope for Derol to have a normal life after all?"

I nodded, although I didn't really like to think of it that way. Seemed like he had a pretty normal life when we were at his home. It was only in school where things got flaky, and that was only because of a small number of idiots.

"Hey," I said, an idea arising in my mind as suddenly and mysteriously as Sally Jean in the mirror.

Jase stopped. We were almost back at the barn where Billy and Derol were still deep in conversation. "What?"

"Maybe you can try your mom again. Ask her about Sally Jean? She might not have been at the dance, but surely she heard about it. Everyone knows everything in Crossroads, right?" I tried not to sound too eager. I knew how little Jase and his mom communicated lately.

"Sure," he said. "I can try. Nothing ventured—"

"—nothing gained."

He laughed and tugged the end of my braid.

"You think he'll let me b-back on?" Derol asked as soon as we were back in earshot. "What s-spooked him? It wasn't something I did was it? I th-thought I was doing great—" Derol's eyes were shining, but his head was jerking just a bit, and his right leg had taken to kicking out sideways every now and then.

"You were doing great. I think Buddy thought someone said the word supper," Jase joked. "That horse is a glutton, let me tell you. Don't even think of saying the word o-a-t-s in front of him. Always spell it, otherwise he'll scrape you right off going into his feed stall."

Derol threw his head back and guffawed.

Buddy jerked his own head up and looked at the new boy as if he'd lost his mind. But he stood still and allowed Derol to climb back on. It helped that Billy was stroking his nose and walking along beside them. Jase was leading, and Derol was holding the reins and the saddle horn again. I climbed up on the fence and enjoyed the view. It made me feel good inside, seeing Derol happy like that. Especially since Billy Bob was here, too. The more the merrier. The more friends he makes, the better off we'll all be.

18

When everyone was tired of riding, we unsaddled Buddy, brushed him thoroughly, and gave him a coffee can full of oats. Jase was right. That horse was a glutton. He almost took my big toe off when he stepped on my foot trying to get past me to the feed trough.

"I love that horse," Derol said simply.

We all laughed and agreed with him. I loved the way Derol said whatever was on his mind. It was so different from the other kids in school. Except for us, the three Mouseketeers, we didn't really hide anything from each other anymore. Until now, that is. I decided it was a good time to tell Billy everything that was going on. It had all happened so fast, we hadn't told him about Sally Jean, or even about encountering Fred at the old school.

"Hey, you guys." Everyone was standing around in the barn, listening to Buddy munch his oats. They all stopped and looked at me expectantly.

"I, um, well, never mind." Maybe I should wait until we were alone. Then I thought again. If Derol is going to be one of us, he needs to start opening up a bit. "Yes, I do want to say something, after all." I tucked my braid in the corner of my mouth and found a seat on the top rail again.

"What is it, Stevie-girl?" Derol asked seriously. That was the first time I'd ever heard him use my nickname. It made me smile.

"I was just going to tell Billy what happened that day we went to the school house because we thought you were there..." I clamped my mouth shut. I just couldn't come right out and tell Derol about Sally Jean. He hadn't been here last year. He might think we were all nuts.

"It's okay," Billy said. "Me and Derol were talking about that day. I told him I was sorry someone tripped him, and he said he was sorry Fred poked me in the eye and started the fight at the game last night. He seemed to think it was all his fault, somehow." He grinned at Derol who was bobbing and weaving in a stray shaft of sunlight falling through the haymow. The weather was still overcast, so that bit of sun was very welcome. Billy continued, "We both agreed that A) Fred is an idiot and B) we aren't going to let idiots ruin our lives."

"Wow, you been eating your Wheaties or something? Sounds like all those vitamins are going to your brain." Jase said it jokingly, but I understood what he meant.

This was so unusual. Billy was usually just sort of there. He seldom took the initiative to solve things this way. I was so proud of him. I felt like his mother.

"So," I said, getting back on topic. "Did you see Fred and his brothers inside the school that day?" I directed my question at Derol to let him know we were certain he was in there.

Bobbing and weaving, he took a long time to answer. "No. Remember, I heard someone. But I never saw who it was."

"That's right, you did tell me that. I just thought maybe you'd left something out."

Jase saw where I was going. "You mean, like the lock that was there and then wasn't there?"

I nodded. Derol stopped bobbing. "You s-saw that, huh?"

We explained what we were talking about so Billy would understand.

"Wow," he exclaimed. "So that's where you've been hiding out when people, I mean idiots, get on your nerves?"

Derol grinned. "Yep. The first d-day, I ran home, but my mom w-w-wasn't there. She was in her n-nursing class, and I didn't have a k-key to the house yet, so I just w-went exploring. Found the open door to the old school. The broken l-lock was just hanging there. I saw those words in the d-dust."

That was the most I'd ever heard him speak. We all sat, stunned, for a second or two.

Then Billy piped up. "What words in the dust?"

I waited to see if anyone else would explain. When they didn't, I said, "Someone wrote help me on the dusty floor of the old elementary. We could see it through the front window."

Billy started toward his bike. "I gotta see this," he said. And I believe he would have gone on with or without us.

"Wait up," I cried. "Derol and I have to get home. We'll ride with you."

Jase caught my arm as I leapt off the fence. "Can we go to the library later?"

"Sure," I said. He was still holding on to my arm. Why did that make my breath catch-up in my throat? Was it because he was so close and my back was against the fence? I stood perfectly still, waiting to see if he would say something else, but he didn't. He just gave my elbow a little squeeze and then turned and headed for his bike. But I saw him flip his hair back as he turned away.

We were nearing the old school when it dawned on me that

Derol had admitted seeing the words in the dust. That meant that he had not written them as I had first suspected. So it was most likely Sally Jean. That would explain her appearance in my mirror—she needed help just like the phantom pilot had needed help. But it didn't explain why she needed help after all these years. Unless the broken lock had something to do with it. Had Fred and his brothers been in there before Derol? But why would that bother a phantom?

A lighting bolt struck me between the eyes: She was frightened because Fred was the son of one of her original tormentors. So much for Jase's no-such-thing-as-a-coincidence theory. I thought that was one heck of a coincidence. Or Fate. Could it be Fate bringing them together through Derol somehow?

By the time we got to the school, my head was spinning just like the spokes on my bike wheels. Thankfully, it wasn't late in the day like it had been the last time we were here, but it was cloudy and overcast. That made the shadows just as deep under the archway.

We all jumped off our bikes and rushed up to the front window. Sure enough, the words were still there.

"T-That's what I was talking about," Derol said, pointing.

We all pressed our noses to the glass. "We see it," I said. "Did you put your other bike lock back on the chain?"

Derol nodded. I think he was afraid to admit it, but he headed around the side of the building anyway, with us following close behind. All except Billy, that is.

He was still standing there, face to the glass, when Derol and Jase disappeared around the corner. "Uh, Stevie…"

I recognized that tone of disbelief in his voice. "What is it?" I hurried back to his side and sure enough, there was Sally Jean, doing her twitchy thing right out in the open part of the foyer, right beside the letters.

"I think I know who wrote it," Billy Bob said matter-of-factly. "I know that little girl isn't of this earth—"

His choice of words almost made me smile, but only because I was already so used to seeing her. "What makes you say that?" I asked, thinking he would say it was her pale skin or old-fashioned clothing.

"Look," he replied, pointing. "Her feet aren't even touching the floor."

I looked closely. They weren't touching. They were several inches above the floor, and they were shaking along with the rest of her body. Next, her eyes will roll up, and she'll fall... She didn't disappoint me.

"Ohhh," Billy let the word out on a sigh. "That's awful. What's the deal?"

I forgot it was his first time to see her death scene. It was awful. Terrible. But he simply accepted what he'd seen without question. Of course, he'd been in on the whole final scene with the phantom pilot last year, so I guess it was to be expected. Still, even I hadn't accepted it as easily as he did. Different strokes, I suppose.

Sally Jean flopped about on the floor like a fish on the bank. "C'mon," I said. "She does that a lot. But not always. Her name is Sally Jean, and she was a friend of my Mom's when they were little girls."

Jase and Derol had removed Derol's bike lock and were just opening the door. "I think she was doing that to test you. I'm surprised she didn't do it in front of Derol... I wonder if he's seen her do that?"

"Let's ask him," Billy said. But I wasn't sure that was a good idea. If Sally hadn't shown herself to him, there might be a reason for that.

Just as we walked inside, Jase said, "What's that?" He was peering around the tall form of Derol who seemed to think he was giving us the grand tour.

Billy and I peeked around both boys and immediately saw it

—more words in the dust. This time they were written in the kitchen floor, right in front of the pantry door:

YOUR SECRET IS LOOSE NOW

The words seemed to leap out of the dust and into my eyes, into my mind. My brain froze for a moment. The words seemed sinister, threatening. "What's it mean?" I whispered.

Derol stopped in his tracks. "She wrote it. T-that little g-girl."

All our eyes went to Derol's face. "You've seen her?" I asked.

He nodded. "She tries to h-hide from me, but I see her t-turning the corner sometimes. I think she doesn't want to s-scare me." His stutter was getting worse as he gazed off through the shadowy confines of the kitchen. "She li-lives here."

We'd thought we were protecting him from her, and she was trying to protect him, too. And all along he was wise to everything. Sheesh. As usual, there was way more to this boy than any of us realized.

At that moment, the door to the pantry popped open with a groan.

We all jumped. Even Derol. The only thing is, he didn't stop.

The door stood open a few inches, a slice of darkness leaking out. The four of us were rock still, holding our breath—okay, Derol was almost still—and yet...I leaned closer. Was that a sigh I heard? I searched Jase's face to see if he remembered the breathing coming from the pantry before.

In response, he grasped the edge of the door and pulled gently.

Cr-e-e-e-a-a-k.

It sounded as if it hadn't been opened in an eternity. I slapped my hands over my ears. Billy Bob's mouth was open almost as wide as his eyes. Derol was dancing on one foot, his elbows doing their best to touch behind his back. His head was jerking and his mouth was turned down in a grimace. Seeing that, I wondered if we should just hightail it out of there before he imploded, but before I could voice that thought, Jase reached out and yanked the door the rest of the way open.

Scrrrack!

We all crowded around to see what we could see.

"It's so dark," I whispered. "I can't even tell how big it is—"

Jase ducked his head and stepped inside. His voice echoed when he said, "It's big. But I can't see a—ow!"

It sounded as if he'd banged his knee, or maybe his shin.

"You okay?" My voice was louder this time, but not much.

"Stay there," he said. "I've found somethi—" His voice cut off suddenly, without explanation.

"Jase!" I started into the pantry, but Billy was there first. He put his hand out. I stopped.

"Hey. You all right?" He listened intently for a response—we all did.

And then we heard it, the sound of breathing. It was almost like a breeze through pine needles, a sighing sound from way back in the pantry. How big was that space? I immediately thought of Narnia, the land beyond the wardrobe.

Billy Bob disappeared into the black.

"Wait." I didn't want to be left alone. I'd forgotten about Derol.

"D-d-don't go in there," he said. He was hopping now, and his arms were flapping. I thought of Gramps saying they used to call Mayor Stone Chicken Little.

"I'm not going in, Derol. We will just wait out here..."

That's when Sally decided to reappear. She stepped out from behind the open pantry door and pointed inside. Then her head fell over to her shoulder, her eyes rolled up, and she began to twitch. Derol took off toward the little hallway.

"Wait," I called again. But I wasn't sure if I was talking to Derol or Sally Jean. Both I suppose. "Come back."

Derol stopped in his tracks, skidding a bit in the dust. I

looked down at the words again. Your secret is loose. What could it mean? Had something—or someone—been locked in the pantry? Had Sally Jean been locked in the pantry the night she disappeared? Chills coated my flesh like a cloak of ice. I stuck my head into the darkness and almost had it taken off by Billy Bob rushing back out.

"Jase fell in a hole." His eyes were rolling almost as wildly as Sally Jean's. "I need a light. I can hear him..."

"C'mon, Derol," I commanded. "We'll ride to my house for a flashlight."

He didn't argue, just took off down the little hallway and right on outside where we were both surprised to find that it was still afternoon, but dark. The clouds had coalesced into a single huge blue-black umbrella directly over our heads. The smell of rain rode the air like a damp perfume and we both inhaled deeply as we jumped on our bikes and lit out down the road.

Gramps wasn't home. I raced inside, grabbed the flashlight from the junk drawer, checked to make sure it worked—wonder of wonders, it did—and then Derol and I started back toward the school. We'd made the four blocks to my house in record time, with Derol leading the whole way.

But it was all for naught.

When we slid back into the weedy lot at the side of the school, Billy Bob was leading Jase out of the door. Jase was holding his head with one hand.

"Are you okay?" I slipped off my Stingray and let it fall to the ground.

Jase nodded gingerly. "Yeah, I'm all right, I just took a wrong step, went down a flight of stairs. Hit my head."

I was immediately reminded of his fall down the stairs in the old Taylor mansion when we discovered the truth about Rennie Taylor and Mr. Pearcy's brother.

"There are stairs in the pantry?" I looked back at the still-open kitchen door. "Why?"

"Some kind of storage room or something," he said. "Smelled like dirt."

Together, Derol and I said, "A cellar."

We looked at each other in awe. "Jinx," I said, holding out my pinkie finger. "You owe me a Coke."

Derol looked at me like I was crazy. Guess they didn't pinkie-swear in the Philippines. He crooked his finger and hooked it in mine anyway. We shook silently.

"A cellar in a school?" Billy Bob asked. "Why?"

I shrugged. "They had to go somewhere in tornado season. Besides, I'll bet they kept their potatoes and apples down there. Remember, it was built around the turn of the century, before they had trucks to bring in food every week."

Billy nodded sagely. "I guess so..."

"It's a cellar all right," Jase said, still rubbing his forehead. "I don't know about fruits and vegetables, but something was down there."

That shut us up.

"What do you mean?" My voice was tiny.

"That noise we keep hearing, like breathing?" He looked at me, his clear green eyes watching mine.

I nodded at him to go on.

"It's down there."

My stomach clenched into a knot of dread. "What? What's down there?"

He stood slowly, and looked around. "Sounded like a draft, just a tiny draft coming in from the outside somehow. Like a door cracked open or something. But I couldn't see any light at all."

Whew! I relaxed a bit as he began to poke around in the weeds like he'd done the day we looked for the chain.

"Help me look for another door or something. Flat, or almost flat, on the ground. You know, a cellar door."

Ahhh. That made sense. Soon, we were all walking around, pushing weeds aside with our feet.

"Be careful," Jase said. "It sounded like wind was coming in through a crack or something. If you step on the door, it could cave in." He touched a spot on his forehead when he said that last part. I wondered if it had made a lump.

"Why are we looking out here?" I asked suddenly. "I've got the flashlight. Let's go back inside and look around. We could probably spot it right away."

"F-found it," Derol called. "Here it is." He was standing near the wall, a look of triumph on his face.

We all rushed over and there they were, set almost flush with the ground, a set of rusty-looking metal doors. Even rusty, they still appeared to be somewhat newer than the rest of the building. My guess was the school district had replaced the old wooden doors with these somewhere along the way.

"Nothing's getting in there," Billy said, pointing to the place where the two doors had been welded together.

"Or out," Jase added solemnly.

That gave me the creeps, and I hugged myself just as the first drops of rain began to fall. For a moment, I was certain we were about to be assaulted by balls of gray goo again, but no. This was simply a good old Texas rain, sudden and severe.

"Lock it up, Derol," I called as we headed for cover under the overhanging arch.

Derol slapped the chain and bicycle lock on the kitchen doors just as the rain became a deluge. "Looks like it's gonna be a frog strangler," I yelled, quoting one of Gramps's favorite expressions.

"Or a gully-washer," Billy yelled back cheerfully.

When Derol had the lock in place, we all ran under the overhanging archway in the front of the school, but the wind had kicked up, and soon it was slashing underneath the overhang in sideways sheets.

"Should we make a run for my house?" I shouted.

The boys shook their heads in unison. "It'll let up in a minute," Jase mouthed. The sound of the rain on the old roof was as loud as the actual thunder that shook the sky and made us all yelp. I imagined it was like being inside Jase's bass drum. We had to yell to be heard, even standing right next to each other with our backs to the windows, huddled up against the chill. I wanted to turn around, face the windows.

I was certain I could feel Sally Jean standing just behind us on the other side of the glass, but I didn't. I couldn't make myself. For some reason, knowing about the cellar frightened me more than anything I'd seen so far.

19

Even though the rain finally did let up, it was still coming down softly, and we were drenched by the time we got home. In a way, it was good. Derol and I both had excuses for being late.

Jase and Billy went on once they escorted us home, but I felt a little off somehow. I wanted to know more about what Jase had seen down in the cellar, and what had made him fall to begin with, but as usual, things had happened so quickly that we hadn't had a chance to talk.

I was glad when the phone rang after supper.

I pulled the receiver into the utility closet where I snuggled up with the broom, the mop, and the ironing board so I could talk to Jase in private. Not that we ever said anything earth shattering, but still, it was nice to be able to talk without wondering what Gramps was thinking about my side of the conversation.

"So," I began. "Can you believe Derol can see Sally Jean? I thought we were the only ones, I mean besides Billy Bob, of course. Because of what happened last year, you know?"

Jase was quiet for a minute. "I hadn't really thought about it," he said at last. "But I guess I sort of felt like we were the only ones, too."

I had my braid stuck in the corner of my mouth, thinking. "Do you suppose there's any truth to that old rumor about why our town is named Crossroads?"

"Rumor? What rumor? The settlers built it at the crossroads of two old cattle trails, that's all. It—"

"No, no, not that one. I'm talking about the rumor about the town being built at the site of the place where the wagon trains crossed over a major Comanche trade route, that crossroads. I mean, there must have been a lot of violence, right?"

I could hear the tease in Jase's voice when he spoke. "Hadn't heard that one." He let out a chuckle. "Let's not stretch things too much—"

"Stretch things," I hissed. "How can we possibly stretch things any further than they already are? We're all seeing Sally Jean. It isn't just us anymore. What's going on?"

"Stevie-girl? Everything all right?" Gramps must have heard me raise my voice.

I clamped my hand over my mouth. Sometimes I got carried away. I removed my hand and called out, "Fine Gramps, just arguing with Jase as usual..."

I heard him laugh. Sometimes I thought the reason he liked Jase is because he wasn't afraid to tell me when he thought I was wrong. Gramps said it kept me from getting too big for my britches. I didn't like to think about that. It was apt to make me mad.

"Keep him in line," Gramps joked. Then I heard him get up and go over to the TV and turn the volume up a little higher. It sounded like he was watching Red Skelton, one of his favorite comedy shows. He loved when Red Skelton played the character of Clem Kadiddlehopper or Freddie the Freeloader.

"Well, if you don't want to talk about the Comanche, then

tell me what made you fall down those stairs." I twisted the long phone cord around and around my finger as I waited for him to answer. In a moment, the tip of my finger turned dark purple. I poked the swelling tip experimentally, but then I freaked out and unwound the cord as quickly as possible. The pink rushed back into my finger even before I was done unwrapping. "Jase?" I realized he'd never answered.

"It was just so dark," he said quietly. "I opened that door at the far end of the pantry, and I thought I was stepping into another storage area. Instead, I went down. It was only about a dozen steps though."

"Oh man. Did you hit your head on the stairs or on the floor at the bottom?"

"On the stairs, I think. Though they are really more like wooden steps. Old, you know? The first one was gone, or broken, or something. You know what they say...watch that first step, it's a lulu."

I laughed in spite of myself. "What is it with you and stairs?"

Jase laughed, too. "Just clumsy, I guess."

"Thank goodness, you're okay. You are okay, right?" I tried not to sound mother-hen-ish, but after hearing that he'd fallen all the way down, it made me realize how lucky he'd really been.

"I'm fine. You still wanna dress up like Outsiders for Halloween?"

And that's how he always did when anyone expressed concern for him, he changed the subject. Guess we had that in common, too.

"Yeah," I said. "If you do...I kinda feel like we're living our own weird little novel here, not The Outsiders necessarily, but something. I mean, the Socs and the Greasers paralleled each other's lives like the settlers and the Comanche, and when the two groups crossed each other, something bad always happened. Sort of like us and the spirit world."

Jase piped up, "Yeah, I get what you're saying, but in our case, the something bad has always happened before we cross paths with them."

I leaned back against the ironing board, making it squeak, absorbing this statement, and I had to admit it. He was exactly right.

"I've got another parallel for you—" he said in the gap.

I waited.

"Bullies and freaks."

"Jase!" I couldn't believe he'd said that.

"Not my word, I'm just parapharasing. And I wouldn't say that to anyone but you. But wouldn't it make a good title for that novel I'm going to write someday? I know you understand what I'm getting at."

"I guess I do," I said. "But which of those groups do we fit in, you and me?"

"We're the outsiders," he said. "Just like Ponyboy and Cherry in the book. They didn't really fit into the Socs or the Greasers... they were kind of like us, on the fringe. And Billy, too, I guess. He doesn't really fit in any of the other groups. Even if he is a jock."

"You know, I used to feel like it was a bad thing, not fitting in. Now, I'm not so sure."

Jase was quiet. I admired the way he always stopped to think before he spoke. I needed to practice that. My temper often put my tongue in gear before my brain was ready.

Finally, he said, "To a lot of people, we're probably freaks."

"That's okay with me," I replied. I pictured him sitting there on his bed with the phone pulled off the hallway shelf and into his room. He showed me once how the cord was just long enough to stretch from the little niche in the hall, around the corner and into his doorway. Then he could slip the cord under the edge of his door and we could talk privately. His folks were strict, though. He could only talk for twenty minutes at a time. They were always afraid someone might be trying to call them about Rusty or something.

Sometimes it scared me, the way I'd already incorporated Jase into my life. Besides my Gramps, Jase was the only person I talked to. Really talked to, I mean, about stuff that mattered, like bullies and freaks and death. Of course, I talked to people and teachers in school, and Billy and now Derol. And I still wrote to Karla every couple of weeks, but that was just surface stuff. With Jase it was different. We talked about the underneath topics. But sometimes that was hard to do in twenty-minute increments.

SUNDAY WAS a lazy day with just Gramps and me cooking breakfast together and trading sections of the Sunday paper as we ate. I didn't even speak to any of the guys, and even Sally Jean seemed to have taken the day off. I used the time to work on our class project on The Outsiders, making a timeline like Jase and I had talked about, and I also had time to go through Mom's closet to see if she had any clothes that would be suitable for Cherry Valance.

The next day at lunch, the four of us gathered at our table. I jokingly asked the group if they realized that Derol was the fourth Mouseketeer, and Billy argued that the original Musketeers, the real ones, only had three members. I told him to actually read the book, and he looked at me so comically when he said, "What book?" that we all burst out laughing.

Actually, I hadn't read it, either. Jase is the one who had told me about it. I think he'd read every book in our school library, but then, he was a year older than me. I still had time to catch him, maybe.

The weather was so gorgeous. Puddles from yesterday's storm had almost prevented us from being allowed to eat on the patio, but Mr. Terrance had relented at the last minute. I think the sparkles reflected in the puddles stippling the cement made him realize the fresh air was better than the stale cafeteria air, even if it did smell of yummy lasagna.

Then, as if in a nightmare, Fred appeared from nowhere and sauntered slowly by our table. "You cost us the game, freak lover!" He spat the words at Billy, but his eyes shifted to Derol as he spoke.

I heard the words, and I saw them, too. I saw them as they had been written in my mom's old yearbook. FREAK LOVER! And I wondered if Fred's dad was the one who had written them so long ago. Like Gramps said, that apple didn't roll far from its seed.

Billy raised his head and looked Fred in the eye. Derol stood abruptly, his left arm lashing out in response to the sudden wall of tension. Billy stood, too. He was of medium height, and wide. Derol was tall and solid, but Fred was tall, wide, and solid. He turned around and sauntered back toward our table, arms cocked at his sides like John Wayne advancing on a bad guy.

"I'm n-not a f-f-freak!" Derol said. His knee jumped so hard it smacked the edge of the cement table, and I felt a sympathetic twang in my own knee.

Never taking his eyes off Fred's face, Billy swung one leg over the cement bench. I was afraid we were about to have a repeat of the episode during the football game.

Jase slid off our stone bench cautiously. He was taller than all of them, but lanky. I felt like an extra in a bad movie. Should I try to run inside and grab Mr. Terrance before the fighting started? I looked at the double doors to the cafeteria. The distance from here to there appeared to have multiplied like the crazy-perspective room at the state fair—no matter how long you walked, you never got to the end of the mirrored hall.

Then Sandy appeared.

Uh, oh. No way we could take Fred and Sandy both. Especially since the quarterback always had a couple of teammates stuck to his heels like oddly shaped shadows. I glanced around and sure enough, there they were. Jip Garza and Kenny Burdett lurked casually on the edge of my peripheral vision.

I glanced at the double doors, gauging the distance once more. Could I make it? The rest of the kids suddenly stopped talking when they realized what was about to happen. The silence was as thick as the smell of last night's rain.

Sandy looked at Fred, but he planted his palm on Billy's chest and I thought Billy was going to come undone. I swear I saw steam shoot out of his ears. But what with Sandy being the quarterback, it was like he had some sort of control over all his players.

"Sit," he commanded. And he gave Billy a little shove. Derol's arm flew out, and I could sense him getting ready to leap.

"We're gonna put an end to this crap right now." Sandy's voice carried as if he had a bullhorn in his larynx, just as it had on the field Friday night.

Fred relaxed, a sly smile curling his lip. He was certain he'd won. No one would go up against Sandy. He was the definition of the BMOC—big man on campus.

"You cost us the game," Sandy said. And although he still had his hand firmly planted in Billy's chest, it was apparent his words were directed at Fred. "If you hadn't given Billy that black eye and got him benched, I wouldn't have got sacked, and we probably would have won." He stared the other boy down, daring him to deny it.

Fred's face grew tight, his eyes got small, and I saw a look there that reminded me of the neighbor's dog—the one who'd been taught to sic everything that happened into his yard. It was a terrifying look. "Can't believe you're defending this freak lover," he said. "When you were the one making fun in the locker room..."

Sandy's face reddened, and he glanced at Derol. "I did, and I shouldn't have." I think that was his version of an apology. "I never realized it would affect the game." Ahh, there it was. It had begun to affect sports.

Fred made a sound of disgust, and then turned on his heel to stalk off toward the building. When he got out of the line of site of the double doors, he looked back at us, stopped, and spat on the ground.

I felt a light touch on my back, like a finger twinging a bowstring, and I almost leapt over the table myself, but it was just Missy. She was actually smiling a little, as if she'd been on our side all along. Wait, wasn't she the one standing there that day Derol was tripped? What was going on here? I sat back down with a thud. But I wasn't hungry anymore. The lasagna smelled like dirty dishwater now. At least the other kids had begun to chatter again. They sounded like a covey of quail after the hunter has gone.

Missy made her way around the table, and without another word, she and Sandy linked hands and strolled off as if nothing had happened. I felt as if a wet blanket had been thrown over the entire day.

"Well, that was bad," I said to no one in particular.

Jase patted my back in sympathy. "Not too bad," he replied under his breath.

I jerked my head up. How could he think that scene wasn't bad? It had been horrific to me. Was it one of those guy things? They certainly didn't seem to be as bothered by the threat of violence as I was, but that wasn't what Jase was talking about at all. He inclined his head at Derol and Billy Bob. They had both sat and were digging into their food like there was no tomorrow. "He didn't even think of running off," Jase murmured.

He was right. Not only had Derol not run off toward home, he had actually stood up and told Fred and the whole world he was not a freak. Wow. And I had dismissed the entire thing from my mind simply because they had almost come to blows. Maybe it was a guy thing. "That took courage, didn't it?" I whispered back.

Jase nodded. "I think he finally believes he can count on us."

Of course, that's what it was. After the incident with Buddy, and then inside the old school, he finally learned we could be trusted. The wet blanket lifted and the light began to pour into my world again.

20

"It's almost here," I told Jase after we'd waved goodbye to Derol. He'd ridden home with us and we'd left him on his doorstep. "Have you got your outfit all ready?"

He laughed. "You mean my Ponyboy costume?"

"Yes," I nodded. "Or Sodapop..." I had to tease him a little, because I was just so glad he wasn't backing out on me. I'd already bought the temporary red hair dye and dug through Mom's closet for my own outfit. I was actually beginning to look forward to it, the dressing up part, I mean. Even Derol was getting excited. Ever since the near-altercation at lunch, he'd been jabbering almost non-stop. I noticed his stutter was starting to abate also. I think it was being replaced with speed talking.

"What do you think Derol is going as?" I asked, recalling how he'd said he had a surprise in mind if his mom could help him.

"I can't wait to find out," Jase replied. "It could be anything." He cocked his head to one side so that the hank of hair fell out of his eyes. "I wonder if it has something to do with his Filipino heritage?"

"That's a thought." I got off my bike and pushed the kickstand down with my foot. We were headed to Mr. Pearcy's house, but had stopped by for some cookies in my kitchen first. "Maybe he's going to be a dragon or something."

Jase twitched the end of my braid. "That's Chinese culture you're thinking of."

"Hmmm," I said. "Maybe it is. But I think they're related somehow. Something I read somewhere. I'd better do some real research on the Philippines."

Jase laughed and followed me inside. "Any excuse for a trip to the library, right?"

"Right." I said, getting out glasses for milk. "Especially since we never made it there. Oh, I did learn something, though."

He waited, eyebrows raised questioningly.

"I finally thought to ask Gramps if Sally Jean was epileptic or anything. He said she wasn't."

Swiping the hank of hair out of his eyes, Jase said, "Did you tell him why you wanted to know?"

I shook my head vigorously. "'Course not. I just made up some excuse about studying it in school." I poured the milk and brought the cookies to the table. "You didn't get to talk to your mom yet, did you?"

He shook his head. "I can't figure out a way to bring it up without telling her why I want to know." He started down the hall to the bathroom. "Be right back," he said. Then I heard his footsteps halt. "Stevie…"

I hurried to where he was standing. He was staring into my bedroom at Sally Jean. She was standing beside my bed, looking down at Sarey. She appeared not to notice us as she reached out and caressed the old doll.

An ocean of sadness washed over me as I realized that she had probably played with Sarey when she was in this very house, visiting my mom. I started forward meaning to comfort the little phantom somehow, but Jase laid a hand on my arm, stopping me just as Sally Jean stooped down and attempted to pick Sarey up.

The doll slithered to the floor and I gasped, realizing that must've been what happened before—when Gramps and I had heard the book and doll hit the floor.

As we watched, Sally Jean, twitched a few times, and fell to the floor where she disappeared.

We both ran to the spot where she'd been standing. Jase picked up Sarey and gently placed her back on my bed. "Your mom's doll?"

I nodded, pushing a tear from my eye with my knuckles. "We've got to help her somehow," I said. "She needs to go on across the void and be with my mom." I turned and fled back to the kitchen before my voice could break open and spill out all those pent up tears like a breach in a dam. I was thinking about Sally's parents. Gramps said after her death they had moved away. He said he didn't know where they had gone.

We ate our cookies in a fog of silence, and then we headed to Mr. Pearcy's house. He wasn't there, but he'd left a note telling us he'd had to go to the hospital and check on an old friend. He'd shown me long ago where he kept the spare key under the little ceramic turtle in the flowerbed. The note was stuck right in the screen door where we'd be sure to find it. Just do the usual, it read. So we went in and I commenced to sweep while Jase went out back to rake the fall leaves. He said he would also check the gutters to make sure they were still clear. The heavy rain yesterday had knocked off a lot more of the pretty fall leaves.

We were about finished when Mr. Pearcy arrived. His face was grim. "Jase," he said without preamble. "I think you need to go on home, now. Your mom is looking for you."

I felt a cold seed of fear begin to uncoil inside me. I knew something bad had happened. His folks were never looking for

Jase, and besides, he was right here where he was supposed to be.

Jase must've felt the same sense of alarm. He hopped off the ladder he was using to check the gutters, yanked his bike up by the handlebars, and was running down the street with it almost before Mr. Pearcy had finished speaking.

For a moment, I was incredibly hurt that he hadn't bothered to wait for me, or even glance at me before he took off. Surely he knew I would go with him, be with him if something awful had happened. But apparently I hadn't even crossed his mind. Did he know something I didn't?

I looked at Mr. Pearcy to see if he knew anything else. He just shook his head and said he'd overheard a couple of nurses talking. Apparently, one of them was a member of Mrs. Lee's study group.

Mr. Pearcy told me to head on home. I think he could tell my mind wasn't really with the housecleaning anymore, so I didn't argue. As I neared my house, I could see Derol outside in his front yard further on down the block. Was he waving? It looked like he was motioning for me to come down to his house.

"Hey, Derol, what is it?" It was rare for him to make a deliberate spectacle of himself. But the entire time it had taken me to ride the short distance from my house to his, he'd been waving both arms and jumping up and down like a monkey in a cage.

"Where's Jase?" he asked without stuttering.

That seed of cold fear blossomed in my gut. I could feel its icy tentacles threading their way up my veins toward my heart. "Why?"

Derol stopped jumping. He looked toward his house where I could see his mom—a third of her at least—through the open blinds. "Mama's nurse friend told her about Jase's brother—"

I think he was saying something more, but I didn't stick around to find out what it was. His brother, Rusty. Of course.

That was why Jase had taken off like a bullet fired from a gun. He and his family had been expecting this sort of news ever since the day Rusty had gone to Vietnam.

Halfway to his house, I slowed, remembering that I hadn't told Gramps where I was going. I also slowed because the adrenalin was working itself out of my body, and my brain. Would I be intruding if I showed up unannounced? Should I just wait to be called? What if he doesn't call?

I stopped my bike and sat, pondering. The Police Department was only a couple of blocks away. Gramps would be gone already—probably at home worrying about me—but I could stop in and use the phone.

Jelly Wardlow, the evening dispatcher, looked up from his radio when I came through the door. "Why, hello, Stevie. Your Gramps left a half-hour ago."

"I know." I peered over the tall counter. "Could I use the phone to call him so he doesn't worry that I'm not home?"

"'Course, come on around." He motioned for me to come through the little swinging half-door. Then he handed me the receiver and pushed the number three button to give me an outside line. Buttons numbered one and numbered two were for incoming calls only.

"Stevie?" Gramps answered.

"Yes, it's me. Sorry I'm not home, but something has happened to Jase's brother. Mr. Pearcy said he needed to go right home and I was headed over there. Then I wasn't sure if I should so I stopped to call you…oh, Gramps! What's happened? My legs and my voice both went all trembly and I guess Jelly could see I was about to let a faint as Gran used to say, so he rushed around the desk and shoved a rollie chair under my knees. I fell into it gratefully.

"Stay right there," Gramps said. "Tell Jelly I'm coming to get you. Do you hear me?" His voice was stern.

"'Kay," I said, relieved to have the burden of knowledge moved to larger shoulders than mine. I replaced the receiver and told Jelly what he'd said. "Have you heard anything?" I asked, knowing that he'd overheard my side of the conversation.

"About Rusty? No, nothing's come through here." He handed me a paper cone of water from the fountain which I accepted gratefully, but the first touch of that icy liquid on my lips reminded me of how I'd shoved Jase's face into the flow one time when we had stopped by here on a foray to the record store. A feeling of dread came over me. Something awful had happened, I was certain of it. I wondered how it would change Jase, us, our friendship? But then a little voice in my head chided me for being so selfish, for thinking of myself when it wasn't me who was in a crisis.

Gramps was there within minutes. He enveloped me in a bear hug that had me on the verge of tears—I was so glad to see him—and then we went out to the truck after I thanked Jelly for letting me use the phone. He smiled at me and touched his index finger to his hairline in a sort of wave or salute.

Gramps loaded my Stingray in the bed of the truck, and away we went.

"Where we going?" I asked, though I was pretty sure I knew.

Gramps patted my knee. "I called Jase's house and talked to the man who answered the phone. I believe he was a chaplain." He hesitated as he downshifted to make a turn. "Rusty's helicopter was shot down near the front lines."

I knew what that meant. It meant the chopper was shot down near the place where the fighting was most intense. The "front lines" was one of the war terms the news reporters always bandied about on TV. It seemed as if they liked saying certain things like front lines and casualties.

"Is he dead?" I asked bluntly.

"Missing in action," Gramps replied just as bluntly. "M.I.A. I thought we'd just drive on out there and see if they need us for anything."

I nodded, but I couldn't speak. My throat had closed up around a lump of pain the size of a hard-boiled egg.

There were two unfamiliar cars in the Lee's long drive when we arrived. One car had the official emblem of The United States Army on the door. Buddy was at the fence, his head hanging over the top rail, ears pricked forward as if privy to something we couldn't quite hear.

I rushed up the steps and into the house. It felt wrong to be using the front door. I barreled into the living room where two ladies in Sunday dresses, and two men in Army dress uniforms, sat stiffly. "Jase?" I asked of no one in particular. Then I saw him.

He was standing in the doorway of his parent's bedroom, which was just off the living room.

"Mom?" His voice was clogged with concern.

I stepped forward to let him know we had arrived.

I could barely see inside the bedroom. His mom was on her bed, fully clothed except for her good shoes, which were lying haphazardly near the bed. On was pointing one direction, the other pointing the other direction, upside down. Those shoes bothered me. Mrs. Lee was very fastidious in everything she did. The shoes told me a lot about her state-of-mind. In her hands she was holding a picture of Rusty in his uniform.

"I had a bad dream, last night," she was saying as she stared toward the window. The shade was pulled down, but the sunlight glowed through the coated fabric, illuminating the rectangle like a window to the beyond.

"What was it?" Jase asked.

I could see the confusion on his face. He wasn't used to his mom this way. She was supposed to be the one he told his bad dreams to, not the other way around.

For a moment, she was quiet. Finally, she said, very softly, "I dreamed he was calling for me." Her words trailed away as she seemed to run out of air. When she went on, the words were so faint they were like echoes. "He was lost somewhere in a jungle like we keep seeing on the news. He was calling me in his little boy's voice. Like that time we got separated in the department store. You remember?" She looked at Jase, and then smiled wanly. "No, you can't remember. You weren't born yet, and Rusty was only two. He pulled away from my hand and hid in the clothing racks. I couldn't find him anywhere. I finally stood still and listened, and then I heard his voice, just like in my dream. He kept calling 'Mommy, where are you? I can't find you...'"

Jase hurried to the bed as his mother's voice dissolved completely into tears. He sat beside her and patted her shoulder.

I wished his father would get home, so Jase didn't have to do this alone. Mr. Lee was in Lubbock, picking up some new appliance parts from the company's other store.

"What can I do?" His voice was crackly. His hand patting, patting...

I imagined how horrible he must feel, sitting there, watching her try not to cry, but crying anyhow, as if her world had shattered into a million little pieces.

She just took his hand and held it loosely, putting an end to the patting. "It's okay, son. It's all right." She looked into his eyes, her own swimming in tears. "Just forgive me for not being a very good mother lately."

"It's okay—"

She squeezed his fingers to silence him. "No, it isn't. I've been so preoccupied worrying about Rusty." She closed her eyes. "You see, I knew it would come to this. There's been this great hole ever since the day he left for basic training, as if he had already been ripped away, out of our lives."

I saw the moisture on his face. He swiped at the tears angrily. "I know, Mom," he snuffled. "I know." He lay down beside her and I covered them both with the blanket folded at the foot of the bed. When her breathing became soft and regular, Jase opened his eyes and looked at me.

I'd never seen anyone whose face looked so naked, so...skinned.

He got up and we went back into the front room where Gramps was sitting with the church ladies and the military men who had brought the bad news.

The ladies had brought cakes and pies and casseroles. I wondered how they had time to bake them so quickly. Maybe they kept them on hand in a special cupboard labeled food for grief.

After Jase and I came out, the two women went into Mrs. Lee's bedroom. One stayed and the other came back out. She made iced tea and began to heat up a casserole.

"Rusty's missing in action," Jase said to the room at large. "The 'copter he was in was shot down." We all knew this already, but I guess he just had to say it out loud.

He sat on his dad's recliner, and I stood beside him and gripped his shoulder tightly. "Maybe he's okay." I don't know why I said that. I just knew we couldn't give up. Not yet.

Then his dad burst through the front door. Of course, he'd seen the military car in the drive. "What's happened? Is he dead? Is my son dead?" His hair was wild and his shirt was pulled out of the back of his pants. He didn't even have his suit jacket on like he usually did when he was working.

I heard the desperation in his words. The chaplain stood and took hold of him. Mr. Lee was sobbing before he even heard the report.

"Let's go into the kitchen, Stevie-girl," Gramps said. The lady from the church was still in there. Jase stayed seated in his dad's chair. I wanted to stay with him, but I figured Gramps knew best.

More and more friends and family began to arrive until it

seemed the old farmhouse would burst its seams. Gramps shook Mr. Lee's hand, clasped him in a manly hug, and told him not to lose hope. "We're here if we can help," he said. But his dad was in another place. The only one who could seem to reach him was the military chaplain, and he stayed beside him even as he entered the bedroom where Mrs. Lee was sequestered.

I looked at all the well-meaning people, and I knew that Jase's parents were going to be taken care of. I was worried more about Jase than about his folks. He was still ensconced in his father's chair. He hadn't moved, not even when his dad knelt in front of him and assured him that God was watching over Rusty, wherever he was, dead or alive.

Jase nodded when his father said that, but I saw his hands tighten into fists, and I saw him swipe the hair off his forehead angrily.

"We're going home, now," I told him, squeezing his shoulder again just as he had squeezed mine that day in homeroom when he told me the awful news about Janis Joplin. That day now seemed so far away, and so minor compared to this. For a moment, I wished with all my heart that we could start over again, at that day, at that very day. Have a do-over like in a game of kickball.

He reached up and grabbed my fingers as a drowning man might grab a rope. "Stay," he said. His voice sounded hoarse, weary, and old.

Grief will do that, I thought. It will age you in the space of a heartbeat. It doesn't play favorites, and it doesn't take a back seat to youth. It's always there, waiting just beneath the surface of our happiness like the shadow of a giant fish in a slow moving river.

I looked up at Gramps, and he nodded. He was always good about sharing me with those in need. Guess it was because we both had so much experience at losing folks. "Call me when you're ready to come home," he said quietly. "I don't want you riding your bike after dark."

"I will," I said. I thanked him, which sounded really silly after I said it. He just patted me and turned to Jase who looked up as if he would say something, but the silence remained unbroken. Gramps patted him, too, and then he went home alone.

"Let's go see Buddy," Jase said.

He still had an unrelenting grip on my fingers. At that moment, it felt as if he'd never let them go.

We went out the back door and walked toward the barn in the gloaming. The entire driveway was lined with cars. There must've been at least a dozen now. I saw the minister from the Lee's church fling open his car door and hurry up the porch steps. We skirted the vehicles parked on the yellow grass beside the house and made our way straight to the horse. Buddy whinnied softly, his trill carrying on the soft twilight air like the sound of hope, the one with feathers that Emily Dickinson had written about.

21

We didn't talk much, just stood there, rubbing Buddy's velvet nose and the silky spot between his ears. I got the currycomb and the soft brush, and we worked him over in silence. I de-burred his mane and tail while Jase brushed and smoothed his just-coming-in winter coat.

"Can't believe Rusty might be dead," he said at last. "Or worse, a POW or, or he could still be lying out there in the jungle, injured, unable to move, ants crawling all over him, the raining falling on his face, in his eyes—"

I dropped my comb and got to him just as he crumpled to the barn floor. "Shhh," I said, falling to the floor beside him. "Try not to think those things."

He grabbed me and buried his face in my embrace. "I can't help it." His voice was low and ragged. "I keep seeing his chopper going down like all those we've seen on the news and then him—his body—lying there all mangled and those damn ants—"

I pulled him closer, remembering how Gramps had held me

so tightly after Mama died and I kept having nightmares about her trapped in the burning car.

"Shhh," I said again. "Shh..." I didn't know what else to do, so I patted and rocked us back and forth as if he were a child. After a while, Buddy leaned down and snorted his warm horsey breath into our hair and the evening slipped away into full darkness.

At last, he pulled away, scrubbing his wet face on the sleeve of his flannel shirt. "Sorry—" he started to say, but I stopped him with a look.

"It's okay." I tried to stand, but my legs were asleep and unfeeling. I grabbed the middle rail of Buddy's stall and pulled myself up. Needles and pins flooded my feet. I held onto the rail and stomped gently.

Jase reached across the gap that had opened up between us and took my hand. "Thanks," he said.

I squeezed his fingers. "Friends," I said. It was all I could say. I'd meant to say that's what friends are for, but my voice deserted me when I looked at his face in the new moonlight coming in through the wide open doors.

We walked out into the early evening. With the sun gone, the night air cooled quickly. "I'd better call Gramps to come and get me," I said. I didn't want to leave, but I didn't want to go back inside that crowded house, either. Crowds gave me hives sometimes.

"I'll get my license in a couple of years," Jase said. "Then I can drive you home myself."

I liked the sound of that. It made me think he would be around for a while. That didn't happen too often with me. First Daddy disappeared, then Mama died, and Gran, and then Karla moved...best not to start down that gloomy road. If I thought about all the folks I'd lost, then I'd start worrying about the ones I still had, like Gramps. He wasn't getting any younger.

Right before we got to the back door, the one Lady had sprung by pawing it open so many times, Jase tugged at my braid. I turned back to see what he wanted—he was always tugging on my braid—and he pulled me to his chest and held me close.

He pressed his lips to the top of my head and let me go. We went on inside the house, but before I could get through the milling people to use the wall phone in the kitchen, I had to accept a plate of food from Jip Garza's mom. It was loaded with ham, beans, and cornbread. My stomach growled as the smell hit my nostrils and I realized how long it had been since the two cookies in my kitchen after school. She forced Jase to accept a plate, too, and then other adults practically shoved us toward the kitchen table where Mr. Pearcy sat talking with one of the deacons from his church.

When Mr. Pearcy saw us, loaded plates in hand, he stood and offered me his chair. Then he took Jase's plate, set it gently next to mine, and enveloped the head-and-shoulders-taller boy in a silent, unrelenting hug.

The entire kitchen cleared out—except for the three of us— as Jase stood there sobbing onto the shoulder of the man who'd recently lost his own wife. It was as if some bond of grief had suddenly united them, welded them together in sorrow.

I took a few bites of the hot, salty food just to keep my own tears in check.

Mr. Pearcy informed me that he would drive me home since he was about to leave anyway. Then he called my Gramps and told him the same thing. That was one of the best things about my tiny little town. There was always someone around to give you a lift.

By the time I'd finished my plate, Jase had gotten hold of his emotions and finished his, too. He ate with a vengeance and went back for seconds.

Mrs. Garza came and wrapped up slices of chocolate cake for me to take home for Gramps. She gave Mr. Pearcy some, too. He didn't tell her he'd made one all by himself just the day before.

Gramps was waiting for me when Mr. Pearcy dropped me off at the curb. I'd simply told Jase to call me when he wanted to talk. I knew I wouldn't be seeing him in school the next day.

I sat at the table with Gramps as he ate his slice of cake. I was way too full for mine. "I'll save it for tomorrow," I said.

"You okay?"

I nodded.

"How about Jase?" Gramps's blue eyes were keen.

"I don't know. He's taking it hard, but who wouldn't?"

I felt a presence enter the kitchen. The temperature dipped, and there was Sally, staring at me over Gramps's shoulder. Her pale eyes were round and wide. I guess she knew, somehow. It made me wonder if Rusty was dead, and if so, was his spirit wandering the green and black jungle? I'd read that many battlefields of the Civil War era were haunted, especially Gettysburg. If that was true, then what must those blood drenched jungles be like?

I began to unbraid my hair in order to give my mind something else to think about. When I looked up, Sally Jean was gone. But I'd already known she was gone by the way the room warmed up again.

THAT NIGHT, I called Billy and told him what had happened. After we talked, I came to the conclusion that for me, the Halloween dance was off. I knew Jase wouldn't feel like going to a party. I wasn't sure I did either, but I felt bad about Derol. His mom had been working on his costume, and I knew he was excited about it. Plus, he'd made so much headway the last few days that I didn't want to set him back. It still seemed as if the three Mouseketeers were his only friends. And next year was senior high, another new school. I couldn't let him down. I decided that perhaps I should just go ahead and go with Derol. I could still be Cherry Valance. Couldn't let that red dye go to waste.

Billy said he was going. The whole team had been given permission to wear their uniforms to the dance, something that had never happened before. I think the coach was trying to foster some kind of unity among his players or something. Things had been so chilly ever since that day at lunch when Sandy had inexplicably stood up for Derol and alienated Fred in the process. Sandy was the undeniable leader of the team, being the quarterback and all, but Fred had his little group of followers, too. Billy said it was like that old game of Capture the Flag—everyone on the team was divided into two camps, Sandy, or Fred.

IMAGINE MY SURPRISE when Jase arrived at our house for breakfast the next morning. He didn't eat anything, but he was there. Gramps looked as shocked as I felt. But after a moment, I wasn't sure why I had thought he wouldn't go to school—I mean, they didn't have a funeral to plan or anything. What was he supposed to do, sit home and stare at the walls?

I opened the back door and let him in. "You okay?" I didn't mean to ask him that, it just popped out. I guess it isn't just my temper that makes my mouth go without my brain.

"Yeah," he said. "I'm all right." He sat down at the table opposite Gramps who immediately handed him the sports section of the paper.

"Mom and dad all right?" Gramps asked without looking at him.

Before Jase could answer, there came another knock at the

door. I couldn't believe my eyes when I opened it and Derol stood there.

"I was watching for Jase, " he said simply.

I opened the door wider, and he twirled inside.

"Gramps," I said. "Meet Derol Pavey."

Derol held out his hand while standing on one leg. "Nice meeting you," he said as they shook.

"Same here, Derol. Have you had breakfast?" Gramps pretended not to notice anything unusual. I was glad we'd had the talk earlier, about the Mayor and Tourette's.

Derol looked around as if just realizing that he'd entered the back door right into the kitchen. "Yes, sir," he said, but his gaze kept straying toward the remains of the honey buns we'd just eaten. There were two left on the cookie sheet. I'd heated up some extra ones in case Jase did show up, but then he wasn't hungry.

I put one on a plate and set it on the table in front of Derol who was still standing on one leg. Jase pulled out a chair and Derol sat on it gently, as if it was a leaf and he was a butterfly. I thought it must have taken a lot of courage to come down here alone. "How about some milk?" I asked.

Derol looked at me as if I were speaking Martian or something. "I just came to see about Jase." His arm twitched and jumped, but it didn't fly up, and his stutter was completely gone. "I heard what happened." He looked at Jase frankly.

"Yeah," Jase replied. He seemed at a loss for words.

Derol reached across the gulf and touched Jase lightly on the back. Then he turned around and wolfed down the honey bun in two big bites.

Jase grinned. "Thanks, buddy," he said.

And that's how it was decided that we would all be going to the dance together. It was simple really. After all, what could Jase do at home except sit in his room or on the sofa while a steady stream of well-wishers paraded through the house offering condolences and Kleenex. The bad thing was, no one even knew how to console his mom and dad, let alone him. I thought it must be like trying to console the parents of a kidnap victim. You want to give them hope, but you're almost certain hope is nothing but a crippled fairytale. Or some feathered thing that has already flown.

22

I was so excited I could hardly see straight. The temporary hair dye looked perfect. I was so glad Mrs. Kennedy had recommended it. In fact, I liked it so much, I almost hoped it wouldn't wash out too soon. She had been beside herself when she found out we were going as Outsiders. She also made us promise to let her take pictures at the dance so they could be included in the yearbook.

Gramps was another story, though. When he saw me right after I did it, I thought he was going to have a coronary. He literally clutched his chest and fell backward onto the couch.

"Stevie-girl! You gave me such a fright!" His old eyes were gleaming when he said it though, so I knew he was just kidding like always. When he walked into the kitchen, I actually heard him mutter, "'Bout time that girl had some fun."

So I was determined to do just that. Have some fun. Like I said, I was so excited I could hardly see straight, but of course, that didn't mean I could ignore Sally Jean. Nope, she would not be ignored. I could always see her in the mirror. Since she'd taken one day off last Sunday, she was now trying to make up for lost time. The girl never gave up.

When I put the dye in my hair in the bathroom, she showed up twice, just to see what I was doing. She didn't frighten me anymore. Besides, she could never stay very long, or so it seemed.

"Hey," I wrote in the steam coating the mirror. I wasn't sure it would work, but it was worth a try.

"Hi," she wrote back.

I laughed and pointed at my hair. "It's for Halloween." She didn't respond. Why couldn't she hear me?

I thought back over the little bit I knew about phantoms. It was all based on Mr. Gilpin, the phantom pilot. He couldn't speak, but he could hear. Maybe Sally Jean had been deaf when she was alive. No, Gramps would have mentioned that. But come to think of it, she did let an awful lot of us actually see her. Maybe she had become injured before she died, and that's why she couldn't hear. She would always disappear if we surprised her in the school. And I just didn't think it should be that easy to surprise a phantom.

"Can you hear me?" I wrote in the steam.

"Sometimes," she wrote. Then she pointed to her right ear. Her frizzy white hair floated about her head like strands of gossamer.

"Were you deaf in life?" I wrote quickly. She was beginning to twitch, and I knew that meant she would be gone soon.

"No," she wrote. Then she shuddered violently before falling to the floor and out of sight.

This time, just before she fell, I noticed something I'd never seen before. Below her right ear there was a drop of blood. Maybe that meant she could only hear out of her other ear.

I knew this wouldn't go on forever. Phantoms seemed to have limited life spans, if that makes any sense. Mr. Gilpin got weaker the longer he stuck around. I figured that's why Sally Jean appeared to be so much less frightening than before. Or maybe it was simply because I'd gotten used to her.

Before I was finished combing out my new temporary red hair, Sally appeared once more, floating up from the depths of nowhere like black smoke rising from an invisible fire. In moments, she wrote her own message in the steam.

"Hello." She was a girl of few words. Then, before I could write back, she added two more words (a virtual avalanche of letters, for her). This time she wrote, "Your hair?"

Laughing again, I wrote, "Do you like it?" Then I shook my head at the absurdity of the conversation. I finally had a girl to discuss hairstyles with, and she turns out to be a phantom. Be careful what you wish for, I guess.

When she didn't reply, I hurriedly added, "Did you ever have a Halloween dance at school?" I knew I only had a few seconds more before she would begin to twitch and die. I hated that part of her appearances, but I was certain that's what she was showing me. I was pretty certain she had no control over it, either. As if that part of the scene occurred as automatically for her as breathing occurred for me. Maybe it was part of her mission or something.

Sally nodded. "Bobbed for apples," she wrote. She began a new sentence, but she only got a few letters before her hand began to shake so forcefully that all she could make were squiggles. Then she rose up slightly and fell backwards to the floor where, if I could have seen her, I knew she would be thrashing violently. Again.

On the mirror were the letters she had managed to write. "It was my..."

The last two words were illegible. I sure wish she could have finished the sentence.

I thought she might come back again as I was getting dressed, but she didn't show up even though I continued to admire my new red hair in the mirror every chance I got. My hair even felt different. The texture was coarser, somehow, but smoother, too. It made me feel different. More self-confident. Maybe this is why Amber and those other girls wear so much makeup, I thought. It's a form of courage or something. I continued thinking about it as I slipped on Mom's old loafers. I couldn't believe they fit. Guess my feet were growing even if the rest of me wasn't.

I plucked at the collar of the white, button-up shirt I'd decided to wear, and glanced down inside. Nope. Nothing growing there. Oh well, I'd worry about that later. Tonight, I was just excited to be going to a real dance. It would be my first.

Pulling on the bobby sox Gramps bought me at Perry's Variety Store, I stood up and looked in the mirror. "It was my first dance." Is that what Sally was going to write? Or maybe she was going to write, "It was my last dance," or "my only dance." I waited for a moment, thinking she might reappear, but no dice. It was only me, Cherry Valance, looking out of the mirror.

GRAMPS SAID I could walk or ride my bike to the dance with Jase and Derol, but he would pick us up when it was over at ten p.m. If we rode our bikes, he would just throw them in the bed of the truck when he picked us up. It sounded good to me.

This was only the second Halloween that I hadn't gone out trick-or-treating. I didn't go last year because it was the first Halloween after Karla moved, and I didn't really have anyone to go with. This year I was just too old. If you're old enough for a dance, you're too old to trick-or-treat.

Every time some kid knocked on the door all dressed up like a princess or an angel, or even just a little white-sheeted ghost, I ran to get my old plastic pumpkin full of Hershey's miniatures. Everyone loved Hershey's miniatures. It was all I could do to keep from eating one every time I gave a handful to some little trick-or-treater.

I was waiting anxiously when Jase raised his hand to knock on the kitchen door. He had come a few minutes early so I could make sure his costume was as authentic as possible.

Gramps walked in as I was combing the brown grease through Jase's blond hair. He'd brought it with him. I didn't ask him where he got it, and he didn't volunteer to tell me. He just said he had to be Ponyboy, even if Pony was quite a bit darker and shorter. He didn't want to be Sodapop—like I had suggested —because Ponyboy was a runner like him, and also because Pony had such an easy relationship with Cherry Valance.

When he said that, I couldn't argue anymore.

"Besides," he said. "Soda was movie star handsome."

I thumped him on the head. "Yeah, and you're nothing but a frog."

"What in the Sam Hill?" Gramps roared looking at Jase with the messy goo clumped in his hair.

Jase grinned good-naturedly. "Going to the dance as Ponyboy, the Greaser," he said.

Gramps just shook his head, picked up the newspaper from this morning, and retired to his recliner in the living room.

After we slicked his hair straight back, Jase went to my room to change shirts. He'd worn an old tee shirt that already had grease stains from helping his dad change the oil in his car. But he'd brought with him a large brown paper grocery sack that he said contained his costume.

I watched him walk down the hall to my room. The grease made his hair quite dark. He didn't look like my Jase anymore.

I heard a knock on the door and ran to get the candy. A tiny tinfoil robot waited patiently on the porch with his mom.

"Well, what d'ya think?" Jase asked when I walked back into the kitchen. He'd changed into a sweatshirt with the sleeves cut off, and he was pulling on an old denim jacket. He still had on the same worn jeans and tennis shoes, but he'd turned the legs of the jeans up into cuffs.

I smiled. "Perfect!" I said. "Where'd you get the jacket? It's just like the one Johnny loaned Ponyboy, isn't it?"

He nodded. "This one belongs to Rusty. I don't think he'd mind, do you?"

I saw a glint of moisture pool in his bottom lid before he smashed it away.

"I don't think he'd mind at all," I said. "It kind of brings him with us."

Jase pulled a pair of black boots out of the sack, sat on a kitchen chair, and put them on. Then he stood up, and said, "These are his, too." He glanced at the scuffed boots. "Now, it feels perfect."

I clapped as I examined his "outfit." "You are Ponyboy. Except for the height, of course, but I don't think anyone will care about that—"

While I was talking, I was pulling on the soft, butter-colored cardigan I'd found in Mom's closet. It was a little bit big, but my hair really looked red when it fell down across the shoulders of that sweater.

Jase stopped talking, and I felt him staring. I turned around slowly. His face held something I hadn't seen before, but I didn't know what it was.

"They won't notice my height," he said. "No one will even see me."

From the living room, Gramps bellowed. "Let me see those costumes."

I was glad he broke the spell. It was too intense for me.

We hurried into the living room and let Gramps take our picture with his Polaroid Land camera. It had been Gran's camera so I sort of felt like Gramps was letting her in on the action, too. Oh, how she loved to peel the backing off the picture and wave it around while it developed. She always said she was holding a smidgen of magic in her hands when our faces began to emerge from the blackness of the chemically coated paper.

At last, we were ready to go. I hugged Gramps and Jase shook his hand, which made me break out into a bout of nervous giggles I thought would be the end of me, but finally, we got away.

When we went out onto the porch, the next to the last rays of the evening sun were just staining the horizon, and there, sitting astride his big black bike at the end of my driveway, was Frankenstein's monster, Derol. I couldn't believe my eyes. Somehow his mom had turned his skin green, and she'd put something in his hair so that it stuck to his head like a thick black helmet. She'd even fashioned a headband to fit around the back of his neck so that large bolts appeared to be sticking out on either side.

"Ugh!" he said, cracking me up. Then his leg flew up and almost unseated him.

I ran back inside to get Gramps and the camera. I just had to have a picture of the three of us together. Maybe this one would even make it into the yearbook the way Mom and Sally Jean's picture had so many years earlier. That thought gave me a little chill, but you just can't unthink something once you've thought it, no matter how hard you try.

Gramps was happy to oblige my request, but when Derol saw what we were about to do, he began to get nervous. By the time Gramps got down the steps and got us into position, Derol's knee was jumping so that I thought he would shake his bolts right off.

I think it helped to have me there, in between them, because Jase kept up a running stream of nonsense. Who's gonna win the game on Friday, Derol? When did you get that bike? Did you remember to bring your lock and chain? Are you gonna dance with anyone when we get there? He kept on and on so that Derol couldn't focus on what Gramps was doing, and then voila! The shutter clicked and Gramps was pulling the film from the aperture, peeling the back off and waving it gently through the air. I could smell the chemicals on the breeze. It sure got Derol's attention.

When he saw Gramps pull the picture from the camera, he almost broke himself getting over there to see what was going on. I guess he'd never seen an instant camera before. And there we were, the three of us, looking out at the world from a colorful Halloween sunset, me in the middle, and the two boys on either side of me, one tall and green, with too-short pants that had been jaggedly cut almost up to his knees, and the other tall and fair, looking for all the world like a greaser straight out of the 1950s.

The two boys reminded me of negative-positive images of each other. I thought it was very fitting, the way we all contrasted each other. But then Derol's arm shot out and accidentally knocked the picture to the ground.

I hurried over and picked it up. The breeze was mild so it had only blown a few feet away, but the chemicals were still damp and a blade of dry grass was stuck across Derol's face. When I pulled it away, it left a mark on his left cheek, like a light colored chemical slap.

I blew on the picture to finish drying it, even though the directions said Do Not Blow on Picture because you might accidentally spit on it or something. But even when it was completely dry, the mark was still there. I crossed my fingers and drew the sign of the cross over my chest. Then I kissed my thumb for luck. I had to do something to ward off the ominous feeling I got when I saw that mark.

The boys took it from me and examined it closely. Derol

didn't seem to notice anything peculiar, but I saw Jase cross his fingers, too. "Have we got time for one more?" he asked.

Gramps nodded and we lined up again exactly like we were before. This time when he pressed the button, the camera whirred, but nothing happened.

I looked at Jase and he looked at me, and we both crossed our fingers and drew tiny crosses over our hearts. The sun dipped even further below the horizon, and our picture taking session was over.

23

The ride to the school was almost like a fairytale. I was Cinderella going to the ball. I had my prince riding along beside me on a beat-up blue bicycle, and we were dressed like teens from a decade earlier. Maybe he didn't know he was my prince, but just for this night, I could pretend. I'm not sure what part Derol was supposed to play in my little fairytale. It just seemed right that he should be here, too.

Everywhere we looked, jack o' lanterns grinned around stubby candles, or scarecrows made of old clothes stuffed with straw guarded front porches and lampposts. To add to the Halloween ambience, dry leaves scuttled along in the gutters beside us like laughing harbingers of winter, or doom.

Up and down our block and every block we passed, kids hooted and hollered and tripped over one another in their quest to get to the best houses before they ran out of candy. Everyone knew which houses gave out popcorn balls and candied apples and which houses gave out plain old apples or even a handful of walnuts or pecans. And when we passed the old Taylor mansion, there were already a couple of kids daring each other to run up on the porch and try the front door.

When we neared Central Elementary, Derol started pedaling faster. I don't think he even realized he was doing it. When he passed Jase, I had to struggle to keep up. I tried to see if Sally Jean was peering out at us as we passed, but the shadows beneath the archway were almost solid black.

Once we turned the corner, and the abandoned elementary was out of sight, Derol slowed a bit and then we were all riding abreast again. That was good. I didn't want to get all sweaty before we even got there.

We were still a block away when we began to hear the music. The sun was low, but there was plenty of daylight left. The parking lot was packed with cars dropping off kids or parents arriving to chaperone. Everywhere I looked, witches, vampires, and mummies strolled, hopped, and ran toward the gym. There was even a girl dressed like Janis Joplin complete with bell-bottoms, frizzy hair, tie-dyed headband, and round blue glasses. I didn't recognize her, and I didn't have time to find out who she was as we made our way through the throng. It looked as if everyone had come.

There were numerous football players decked out in their uniforms, but I couldn't spot Billy. I did see quite a few flappers though. The 1920s were well represented at the Junior High Halloween dance. I sort of wished I were a flapper. I could almost imagine the cool feel of those sequins flapping against my bare legs. Maybe next year, I thought.

We rode straight up to the racks and locked up our bikes. The music was unbelievable. I kept waiting for a teacher or chaperone to make someone turn down the volume, until I remembered that the band was live. Juanita Silvas had talked her brother, Tony, into bringing his band, The Cymbals, over from the high school. They were ripping into a Buddy Holly and the Crickets medley—That'll be the Day, Peggy Sue, and True Love Ways. I couldn't wait to get inside.

I grabbed Jase by the arm and practically hauled him through the door. Derol followed behind. I caught a glimpse of his face when I turned to make sure he was behind us, and I'd swear that boy had stars in his eyes. His mouth was turned up in a big old Texas grin that was almost as wide as my own.

Jase stopped just inside the door to take in the decorations. We, the members of the band, had outdone ourselves—we had worked for hours after school.

Black and orange crepe paper streamers twirled down from the ceiling of the gym and cottony webs and plastic spiders festooned every corner. Black paper bats swooped and fluttered every time a breeze blew through the open doors.

Everywhere I looked, a mummy lurched, or a witch pranced. But these were the silliest monsters I'd ever seen. Derol fit right in with his green skin, bolted neck, and ragged pants. I was glad the music was so loud. I had some idea that it would be such a distraction for Derol that he wouldn't have time to get nervous. Already, I could see a couple of girls looking and giggling. This time, however, they were giggling in a good way, in a I-hope-he-notices-me way that was extremely transparent to everyone except Derol.

"Punch," Jase shouted at me.

We all headed to the concessions table, which was decked out like a graveyard with a huge cauldron of roiling witch's brew right in the middle. "Good idea with the dry ice," I yelled. Jase tipped an imaginary hat to me. We both accepted cups of misty punch from a blond haired girl wearing a gold eye mask.

"Anna? Anna Packett, is that you?"

She nodded shyly.

I couldn't believe my eyes. I think it was the first time I'd ever seen her at an after-school function.

"Great job," Jase said, holding his punch cup aloft.

"Thanks," she replied, dipping her head as she reached for another cup to fill.

Carrying our drinks high to avoid collisions with other kids, we found a table near the wall. All the gym doors were propped open for ventilation, and the sight of the setting sun through the open double doors gave me a sudden feeling of gloom. I think it was because the quicker the sun went down, the closer this night was to being over. Or maybe it was just that on-the-cusp-of-something feeling. I sort of still wanted to be out running the streets, trick-or-treating with the little kids. But another part of me, an even bigger part, wanted this wonderful nearly-teenaged-night to go on and on. Leave it to me to worry about something ending before it even got started.

As I sat, gazing out the wide doors, I caught movement from the corner of my eye. The band was playing Crimson and Clover, by Tommy James and the Shondells, and they weren't butchering it too badly. Jase was standing beside me, hand out. "They're playing our song." He laughed at his inside joke. "You ready to dance?"

I gulped my punch and stood shakily. The first time we'd heard this song together, the phantom pilot had caused the record to fly off the turntable and whack me in the forehead. But this...this was what I'd been looking forward to, so why was I suddenly so timid?

Jase took my hand, and before I could even think, we were out in the middle of the dance floor, surrounded by monsters and flappers and football players all laughing and dancing and grinning. This is how it should be. This is what all those books and movies have been talking about.

Juanita, the witch, tugged my hair as she danced by on the arm of a werewolf who looked suspiciously like Terry Koker, a boy who sat behind her in homeroom.

"Love the hair, Red," she shouted.

"Cherry," I said. "Not Red." But I was smiling, too.

Jase raised his hand to someone across the room, and I saw Billy Bob arriving with a couple of other football players decked out in uniforms and pads. At least they'd left their helmets behind.

I waved at Billy, too, and he headed toward the concession table, and then to the general area where we'd left Derol guarding our little spot of calm. When Juanita's brother spied her in the crowd, he burst into a quick rendition of La Bamba by Richie Valens. At the same time, his bass player announced that La Bamba was the official song of hula hoopers everywhere, and then a couple of high school girls were suddenly passing out hoops to every couple.

"This is a contest," the bass player said. "You must pass the hoop back and forth between you, dancing inside it as you do, until the music stops. Then you must both raise it and hold it above your heads until the music starts again. The winners will be the last couple standing."

I was a giggling mess after only a few tries. Jase was so tall I kept hanging the hoop on his head every time I tried to get it off him. He quickly learned to lean down and duck so I wouldn't choke him. Even though we lost all our inhibitions, we didn't win.

The limbo was coming up, soon. That's what I was looking forward to. I'd never done it before and I was eager to try. At the end of the night, the judges would announce the winners of the costume contest. I was pretty sure Derol had that one in the bag. I didn't know about the girl winner, though. There were so many good ones.

When the song ended, Jase pushed his greasy flop of hair out of his eyes and led me back to our table. Billy Bob was sitting with Derol, and Laura Gonzales was standing beside the table looking uncomfortable.

"Hi," I said, hoping to put everyone at ease.

Laura smiled. "Hi, Stevie, love your hair." She was dressed as a flapper.

"I love your dress," I replied loudly. "Do you want to sit with us?" We were all still practically yelling even though the band hadn't launched into their next song yet.

Laura glanced at Derol as though waiting for an invitation. "Yeah, sit with us," Billy Bob said. He reached over to the next table and dragged up another folding chair.

A loud voice said, "What d'you think you're doing?" Even over the sound of all the other kids, this voice carried.

We all looked around for the source.

Fred stood on the opposite side of the table where Billy had just snagged a chair for Laura. No one was sitting there. No one at all.

"What d'you want, Fred?" Billy asked. "You wanna sit with us, too? You lonesome?"

I ducked my head when Billy said that. It felt like he was baiting a bull or something.

"Go to h—" Fred said, but the band ripped into their version of Purple Haze about then, and we didn't hear all of his reply. We didn't have to hear it, though. We all knew what he'd said.

Turning our backs on Fred, the five of us bunched up together so we could hear each other. Laura was in between Billy and Derol, whose head was beginning to jerk, and I was in between Jase and Derol.

"C'mon," Laura yelled bravely. "Let's dance." She grabbed Derol-stein's arm and he looked as if he might fly apart. I could just imagine his neck-bolts flying across the room. Before my mind's eye could see any more, Billy surprised us all by giving Derol a playful shove.

"Go on," he said. "I'll go up and tell 'em to play The Monster Mash so you won't look so out of place."

Derol flapped his arm at Billy—I'm not sure if it was intentional or not—and then he and Laura were dancing. Just like when he was singing, or running, or riding his bike, Derol had few tics when he was dancing.

Then Fred was there. He wasn't dancing with anyone. He was just bulling his way across the dance floor, bumping into anyone who didn't jump out of his way. Jase and I hurried out to the dance floor and positioned ourselves in between him and Derol. It was obvious what his intentions were.

Apparently, we weren't the only ones who noticed. Billy Bob made it a point to stroll through the dancers, too. He headed to the snack table and gathered up cookies and napkins for us. By the time the song ended, and we converged back at our table, Fred was nowhere to be seen.

"Glad he's gone," I said with a shiver.

The dance wore on and the music got even louder and crazier. After the band played The Monster Mash, everyone started requesting other silly Halloween songs like The Purple People Eater, The Witch Doctor, and the theme song to The Addams Family.

We danced every song. Soon we were shiny with exertion. Laura and Derol danced every song with us, and Billy Bob, true to his sporting nature, played the field. He seemed to think it was his duty to dance with every unattached girl in the gym.

The band kept attempting to segue back into more popular music like Hendrix or Creedence Clearwater Revival, but every time they did, another half dozen kids would start calling out for more Halloween music. As much as I loved Jimi Hendrix and John Fogerty, I was kind of proud that the majority of our students would rather be silly than cool. Besides, I hadn't had this much fun since before Karla moved. Even Jase seemed to have forgotten his problems when we were all pogoing up and down to the oohs, eees and ah-ahhs of the Witch Doctor song.

Finally, the band took a break and we collapsed in our chairs. Billy Bob had come out of his shoulder pads at some point in the dancing, and he went in search of Mr. Terrance so he could get the key to the locker room to put them up. "They're too hot," he'd said. "But if I lay them down, someone will steal them and I'll get benched again for sure."

Derol and Laura had volunteered to stand in line at the concession table to bring us each another cup of punch, and Jase and I simply sat where we were, watching others mill around, reveling in our newfound sense of freedom.

"This is great," Jase said, taking my hand. "I'm so glad we came."

I grasped his fingers tightly. "Me, too." It felt like we were actually a couple, instead of just friends.

"Did you see Sally Jean?" he asked nonchalantly.

My eyes must have mirrored my shock, because he laughed right out loud.

"She's here?" I craned my neck in order to see over the heads of all the other kids wandering about, looking for chairs or drinks. "Where is she?"

Jase stood. "I caught a glimpse of her over by the apple bobbing booth."

"I can't believe they actually brought that in this year. Who would want to stick their face in that nasty water?" I was trying to see if she was still there, but I was much too short. "Do you see her?"

"Nah," Jase shook his head. "Just a bunch of football players dunking each other."

"Oh, crud," I said without thinking. "Billy isn't one of 'em, is he?"

Laughing, Jase picked me up and held me above the crowd for a moment. "See anything, shorty?" he asked.

"Put me down," I cried, thumping him on the head and shoulders. "Good grief."

But he didn't really put me down at all, just placed my feet on top of his and walked me back out to the dance floor. The band members had returned from their break and were trying to get in their rendition of Procol Harum's Whiter Shade of Pale.

It was the first time we had danced to a slow song, and I wasn't disappointed when Jase wrapped my arms around his neck and pulled me closer. This is it, I thought. This is heaven.

And then all heck broke loose.

24

From the direction of the apple-bobbing booth, there came a sudden rush of sound. At first I thought it was a tornado, then I quickly realized someone had upended the heavy metal washtub that had been holding the extra bushel of apples, and had thrown it against the wall. The clanging of the metal tub against the brick wall made the most ear-shattering series of metallic echoes I'd ever heard. Apples were rolling everywhere.

I recalled the title of the song the band was playing at the very same moment I saw Sally Jean floating around behind the table where the tub of apples had been placed. What had Gramps said about Sally Jean and Mom bobbing for apples the night she disappeared? I had another moment to wish I'd had time to go to the library and research her disappearance, but between Derol's problems and Rusty going missing, that had just not seemed like such a high priority.

"What's going on?" I asked, still standing on Jase's feet, trying to see.

"Fred," he said.

And then we were moving.

It was only a few steps away from the double doors, but the way the kids had packed up around the apple-bobbing area made it difficult to figure out what was happening. We shoved past a witch and her warlock, then a big mummy stepped out of the way and I heard Laura's voice.

"You leave us alone!" she cried.

Jase pushed through the remaining knot of kids and there they were, Fred, Billy, and Laura. Fred and Billy were squared off as if they were on the verge of Armageddon. Derol was nowhere to be seen.

"Stop it, Billy!" Jase demanded. "You don't want to get benched again."

Without taking his eyes off Fred, Billy replied, "He had Derol in the locker room. I forgot to lock it, so I went back...Derol got in a few licks though—"

Blood was dripping from Fred's nose.

"—then a couple other guys jumped in. I didn't see who—"

Out of the crowd, Sandy Morrison appeared and started toward Fred. Seeing the quarterback and his ever-present side-kicks, Fred broke for the door and disappeared into the night.

Everyone breathed a collective sigh of relief.

"Where's Derol?" I asked.

Billy Bob shook his head, a worried look on his face as two chaperones came running up with Mr. Terrance.

"He took off," Laura said quickly. "I tried to get him to stop, but he was very upset. I think he was bleeding, too."

I followed Jase into the parking lot. Our bikes were still locked to the rack. Derol's was gone. "Think he went home?" I asked.

"I hope so," Jase said. "We'd better go find out."

I hesitated. Gramps specifically told us not to ride home in the dark. "Let me just go inside and call Gramps," I said. "He can check Derol's house on the way here."

Jase was still undecided—I could see it in his face, and the way he flung his head back to get the greasy hair off his forehead. "Okay," he said.

That's when Sally Jean appeared in front of us. She had never appeared in such a populated place before. I was amazed that she had been able to come to the dance at all.

I looked at Jase, a question on my lips, but before I could spit out the words, Sally shivered and disappeared. She appeared a little further away, at the edge of the parking lot.

"She's leading us," Jase said. "I have a feeling she's leading us to the old school. Maybe Derol went there."

I was still uncertain. I did not want to disobey my Gramps, but then I saw something that convinced me we had no time to waste.

Fred's big brother, Ross, ran across the road. He was headed away from us, as if he knew we were coming. We heard a car start up. It must have been parked down the block, out of the glare of the school's lights.

I jumped on my bike and gave Jase the okay signal. "Did you see him?" I asked.

"Sure did," Jase replied. "And you know I don't believe in coincidences."

We took off, but we weren't entirely alone. I could hear voices coming out of the gym. One of them belonged to Billy, and the other to Laura. When I glanced back, I was pretty sure I could see Sandy and Missy, and maybe three or four football players with them. I'd seen a handful of bikes locked up in the rack. I hoped some of them belonged to those players. Sometimes an older brother or sister could be cajoled into driving—the way Ross must've done for Fred.

We have to find Derol before Fred and Ross do, I thought, as my legs pumped the pedals. They could really hurt him.

As if he'd heard my thoughts, Jase stood on his own pedals, leaving me behind.

I wanted to call out for him to wait, but I didn't want him to slow down. I was overheated from all the dancing. The night wind rushing past cooled me quickly.

"Stevie," I heard Billy call. "Where ya headed?"

I turned abruptly and waited for them to catch up. As soon as they were close enough I yelled, "Go back and call my Grampa. Tell him to meet us at the old school. Derol's in trouble."

Billy immediately turned and headed back to the school with Laura. She didn't seem to know whether to stay or go. Billy's teammates were standing at the edge of the parking lot. They appeared to be discussing their options.

I took off again. Soon, I was chilled. Up ahead, I caught a glimpse of Sally Jean flickering alongside the road like a badly tuned TV station. How is she doing that? She must be desperate. I hurried to catch up with Jase. Billy knows where we're headed, now. He'll bring everyone. I know he will.

When I arrived at the school, it looked deserted, but Jase was waiting for me near the kitchen doors. Even from the road, I could see a glint of moonlight from the chain lying on the ground. Derol had to be here. It was his bicycle lock that had been holding that chain in place. Where is his bike? I glanced around quickly. I didn't see it.

Jase held his finger to his lips in a signal to remain quiet then carefully pulled open the heavy door. The dust in the hall was almost obliterated from our previous visits. Up ahead, Sally Jean was rounding the corner into the kitchen.

We crept forward like phantoms ourselves. Every part of me wanted to call out to Derol, wanted to scream his name, but not knowing who might be hiding inside made us remain momentarily silent. I couldn't believe our night had suddenly disintegrated from slow-dance heaven, to this, creeping around in silence, following a phantom.

When Jase let the door close behind us, the moonlight was gone and the darkness was like a living thing breathing down my neck.

I grabbed his arm. "Wait," I whispered. I opened the door, went out onto the little brick apron and picked up the chain so no one could come along behind us and loop it through the doors the way they'd done before. I spied a good-sized rock, so I dashed out and picked it up. I wedged it between the two doors so they wouldn't close all the way. It wasn't much, but it let a sliver of moonlight into the hallway. It was the best I could do.

Jase gave me a thumbs-up, and we crossed through the kitchen and into the cafeteria. We came to an abrupt halt just before we reached the foyer. Sally Jean was standing directly in front of us. She wagged her head back and forth sadly, and then she rose up until her head was even with the partially open transom window. Had that always been open? For just a moment, we saw her as she must have been when she was alive. It was like viewing a very old, very scratchy film. Her lovely white hair was in braids, and she was in her long black dress as always, but what was she doing?

Then I got it. She was showing us how she had stacked up three straight-back chairs, the kind that used to sit behind teacher's desks and in time-out corners, and now she was perched atop the highest chair, trying to maneuver herself through the half-open window.

I knew what I was watching wasn't real, not any more at least, but still, it was all I could do not to rush over and hold the chairs steady.

"She's going to fall!" I whispered to Jase.

He was standing, transfixed, beside me, and even as we watched, Sally began to totter. In desperation, she lunged for the edge of the window. For a split-second her fingers connected just as the ladder of chairs collapsed. I could hear her fingernails scree down the glass as she struggled to grasp something, anything. With a scream that may have been audible only in our minds, Sally Jean's grip gave out and she crashed to the cold, hard tile. Jase and I both heard the horrid fwap when her poor head hit the floor, and then she was twitching and shuddering as a rivulet of blood trickled from her ear and her eyes rolled up in their sockets. Head injury, I thought. Brain injury.

It was all over in a matter of seconds, and then she was still.

We rushed across the now-silent space, but Sally wasn't there. The dust wasn't even disturbed except where we had trod. All that was visible was a rash of frost on the inside of the window.

"Derol!" I screamed, unaware that I was even going to speak. "Derol, where are you?" My voice cracked I was screaming so loudly. The sound bounced back at me like panic in a packed and smoky theater. I was certain Sally Jean had brought us here and showed us her death scene because she was afraid the same thing was about to happen to Derol. There were so many parallels between the two of them—their differences that made them feel like outsiders, the bullying, running back to hide in the school to escape those bullies. That had to be the reason she had come back after all these years.

Jase sensed my urgency. I'm not sure if he understood all the implications of what the little phantom had just shown us, but he obviously agreed with me about the need to find Derol no matter who was listening.

"Derol," he called sharply, his deep voice resonating with authority. "Come on out. It's just Stevie and me. Tell us where you are. No one's going to bother you—" He turned around and looked down the long, dark hallway toward the classrooms.

"Maybe he isn't even here." I was suddenly unsure. "I didn't see his bike outside, did you?"

Jase shook his head, and started down the hall. But Sally wasn't done.

All at once, she began to flicker again, on, off, on, off, just like she had done when she was leading us here from the dance. She looked like a real Halloween specter now. You never knew where she would appear next.

"Stop!" a rough voice cried. "What is that thing? Make it stop!" Fred suddenly stumbled into the hallway, waving his hands about his head as if he'd been set upon by a swarm of angry bees. Sally was right in his face blinking off and on, here and there, in front of him, behind him, now off to the side…

The way he resembled Derol pinwheeling his arms was almost laughable. I thought it was sort of ironic, and I wondered if Sally Jean recognized the similarity.

Every time she would appear in front of him, Fred would swat at her, but she would already be around behind him, looming in and out of the deep shadows.

"Where's Derol?" I demanded, at once shocked and secretly thrilled that Sally was getting a smattering of revenge.

Fred didn't answer. He was too busy dashing around, swatting at where he thought Sally would appear next. "Is it a ghost?" he wailed, almost crying. "Is that thing a ghost?"

"Yes, she's a ghost," Jase yelled. We both glanced up at Sally Jean. We knew she couldn't keep this up for long. And sure enough, even as we watched, she began her sad, shuddering finale. "Now you watch," Jase commanded, forcing Fred to stop and look. "Bullies like you are the reason she died in here all alone when she was just a little girl. Just you watch. Then you tell us where Derol is and maybe she'll let you live."

I could only imagine how the cold essence of the little

phantom felt on his flesh as Sally flickered right in his face and then shuddered and crashed to the floor in front of him.

"Tell us," Jase demanded.

"The basement," Fred squawked. "The old cellar part of the basement..."

We knew where that was. Jase gave Fred a little shove, propelling him toward the kitchen and the pantry. But Fred, having been rescued from the chilly phantom student, wasn't about to give in that easily. He broke from Jase and skittered around the corner toward the little hallway leading to the outside kitchen door...where he crashed right into Sandy, Billy Bob, Laura, and two other players who were just coming inside. Behind them were Gramps and, wonder of wonders, Tank Green. Fred, who was too cool to dress up for the Halloween dance, stood out starkly as the only kid not in some kind of costume or uniform.

"Where you going, Freddie?" Sandy asked, taking one of his arms. "I think your dad wants to talk to you."

Mr. Green stepped forward and took Fred's other arm. Gramps had his big flashlight. He shined it directly on Fred's frightened face.

"Don't make me go back in there with that white-haired ghost," he begged, glancing toward the cafeteria fearfully.

"What are you talking about?" his dad demanded, his own eyes suddenly searching the shadows intensely. When he didn't see anything, he went on. "Billy told us what was going on." He glared at his son. "I think you're just pretending there's something in there so we'll forget about Derol." His face was livid, but his eyes kept straying toward the dark places just outside the circle of the flashlight. "We saw his bike laid over in the weeds. Where is he?"

Fred twisted his arm out of his father's grasp, but he didn't try to run. "In the cellar," he muttered.

Jase and I were already attempting to pry open the pantry door. Like before, it was somehow locked from the inside. "We need the light, Gramps," I said. "The cellar is through here."

Gramps hurried over. He started to hand me the big flashlight, but then he saw that the door was locked. He pulled out his Swiss Army knife, flipped open the screwdriver blade, and in moments he had the old hinges off one side of the door.

Fred stood beside his father sullenly. All the other kids were grouped around us so there was no chance for him to sneak away.

"Is the boy down there?" Tank Green asked.

Fred nodded.

His dad cleared his throat. "Is he okay?" He waited for Fred to answer. "Ross told me about the fight. Said you chased him here and followed in after him."

That got Fred's attention. "Ross squealed?" His voice was venomous. "He shouldn't have done that."

His father spun Fred around. "Yes. He should have. We've had too many secrets. I should have told you boys about this old cellar and what happened here. Maybe then you would have avoided it."

That reminded me of the words written in the dust, the ones about the secret getting loose, and I looked down to see if they were still there. But there had been too many feet. They were gone.

Gramps pried open the door with Jase's help. They'd removed two hinges and that was enough. He ducked and went inside the pantry.

"There's a door back there," I said. I was about to tell him about the broken step beyond that door, but my voice was stopped by the sound of a low moan coming from the dark recesses below.

"Derol," I cried. "Are you okay? Where are you?" I started to bypass Gramps, but he put a hand on my shoulder.

"Wait here," he said, his voice was stern. "I know that cellar. It's the same place we found little Sally Jean."

I opened my mouth to argue. Sally didn't die in the cellar. She had shown us exactly where and how she had died—attempting to climb out one of the high transom windows in the foyer outside the cafeteria—but then I came to my senses. I couldn't tell him that story. I was confused, but figuring out the details would have to wait.

"Thought we closed up that old outside entrance down there, Tank," Gramps said as he shined the light on the door at the back of the pantry.

"We did," Fred's dad replied. "We welded it shut."

Ahh, I thought. So that was the old door we'd seen outside. The one that was almost flush with the ground.

Gramps had gotten to the other door, the one leading down into the cellar. "Then maybe you can tell me how Fred got inside the school." He was shining the flashlight down the broken wooden steps.

"Fred?" His dad inquired.

At first the cowardly bully dipped his head and refused to answer. But then Derol moaned again.

"We're here," I called. "But how do we get down there? Are you hurt?" I couldn't just stand there. I had to get in there some-how. "Lower me in," I said to Jase and Gramps. I sat down and stuck my feet into the dark doorway. I knew there wasn't a top step, but I thought if they held my arms, I could make it down the rest of the steps, provided Gramps would let me have the light. For a moment I regretted dangling my feet into the noth-ing-darkness like that. I was pretty sure Sally wouldn't hurt me, and I knew Derol wouldn't, but what if something else was down there? Something that would grab my ankles—

"You don't have to do that," Fred said finally. "I'll show you the other door."

Gramps turned on Fred and said gruffly, "That boy better not be hurt."

"He fell," Fred said. "I saw him unlock the chain and come inside, so I snuck in through the old outside entrance. When he locked himself in the pantry, he thought he was safe. He didn't know I was already in the cellar waiting on him." He looked directly into Gramps's light. We could all see the fear and truth in his eyes. "But I didn't know about that broken step, I swear. I think he knew, because he was being so careful. When he started down the steps from inside the pantry, I jumped out of the cellar-shadows to scare him." He hung his head again. "I guess that's what made him fall." His voice got even lower. "I just meant to give him a little Halloween scare."

That must have been the point when Sally Jean showed herself to us in the foyer and then led us back to the pantry. She wasn't about to let us leave without checking the old cellar. "C'mon," I said. "What're we waiting for?" I heaved myself up and ran back to the kitchen door and outside. "There it is." I pointed to the general area where I'd seen the other entrance. "But it's welded shut." I whirled around and glared at Fred. "You're lying to us."

In answer, Fred ambled over, took the flashlight from Gramps, and then leaned down and lifted one corner of the door. Rather than opening up in the middle, where we could see that the two halves had been welded together, the entire thing lifted up just far enough to be maneuvered over to one side. Its hinges had been attached to wooden frames that had simply rotted away over the years. In essence, the big, stout looking door had just been lying there, attached to nothing. When he slid it aside, we all heard a whoosh. The noise reminded me of the breathing sound we'd heard the day we first discovered the cellar door inside the old pantry.

We all heard Derol moan again. The beam of the flashlight illuminated earthen steps leading right down into the cellar. It was the same place where Jase had fallen earlier, only this time we were coming in from the outside, not through the kitchen pantry. He must have been in a blind panic running from the bullies in the locker room. And then, just when he thought he was safe, Fred jumped out at him from the darkness.

25

"Here, Stevie," Gramps took the light from Fred and handed it to me so we could go down the steps together. We could see Derol crumpled at the bottom of the wooden stairs across the room. He appeared to be trying to sit up. "Take it easy, boy," Gramps said as he knelt beside Derol. "Billy, take someone with you and run to Derol's house. Bring his mother. She's a nurse. I don't believe we need an ambulance. Do you, Derol?"

Derol carefully shook his green head, but I could tell it pained him to do so. I noticed that both his neck-bolts were gone and his shirt was bloody. I wondered if it was his blood, or Fred's.

"Are you sure, Derol?" I asked. "That must've been a heck of a fall. Looks like you've been bleeding."

He put his hand up to his forehead in an eerie imitation of Jase the day he'd tumbled through that first step. "It was dark," he said. "Got a lump." Then his arm flew up and nearly knocked the flashlight out of my hand. It made me think he was going to be all right. "The blood was earlier." His face was hard to read beneath the green makeup so I couldn't tell for certain, but I thought I detected a note of pride in that last statement. Then he glanced up at the steps behind him. "I think I broke another step."

We all looked up and sure enough, the second step was now broken, too.

Sandy and Jase got on either side of him, and together they helped Derol up the earthen steps and out into the moonlight. They'd no sooner sat him down on the grass than his mom drove up. She flung her car door open and was at his side in a heartbeat. Billy Bob and Laura were right behind her.

Mrs. Pavey had brought her own light, one of those little ones the doctor shines in your eyes every time he gets a chance, and she shined it in Derol's eyes pronouncing his pupils "fine and even." That meant he didn't have a concussion. She gently pressed around the lump on his forehead and said it was good that it had swelled outward rather than inward. "Lot more room for it to swell out here than in there." She tapped his head gently when she said it, and we all laughed. Except for Derol. He didn't seem to see the humor in it at all.

"What about this black eye and swollen cheek?" Mrs. Pavey asked.

I was immediately reminded of the picture Gramps had taken of the three of us before the dance. The picture that had wound up with a grass-mark across one of Derol's cheeks. None of us had noticed this mark. His green monster makeup had pretty much covered it, but then we hadn't been playing the light across his face, either. "You get that in the fall?" she asked seriously.

"N-no, ma'am," Derol stuttered. It was the first time I'd heard him stutter in a while.

"You want to tell me about it?" Her musical voice was kind but firm.

Before he could reply, Tank Green said, "It's all my fault. I should have told my boys what really happened that night, instead of letting them live with all the rumors and secrets. Maybe they would have avoided this place."

I wanted to say, no, you should have taught them not to bully people. Then none of this would have happened. Of course, I could never say anything like that to an adult. What came out instead was, "What did happen with Sally Jean?"

Gramps looked like he wanted to stifle me, but he didn't make me retract my question.

Mr. Green rubbed his stubbly chin with the palm of his hand. He looked like an older version of Ross, his firstborn son. We watched as he twisted his head a bit, as if he had a stiff neck or a bad thought. "Sally Jean had an accident," he mumbled at last.

We all heard the mournful whimper of the wind around the edges of the rotting doorframe. At least I think it was the wind. "Was she locked inside?"

His head jerked up, probably wondering how I knew that. I wasn't positive that's how it happened, but I figured that would be the only reason for her to try and climb out that high window. "We were just having some fun—me and some other boys."

I imagined poor little Sally Jean, white hair neatly braided, long black dress already looking like part of a Halloween costume, calling out an unassuming farewell to my mom at the corner, never dreaming it would be her last goodbye.

When had they started taunting her—as soon as my mom had gone inside and closed the door? Or had they waited until she was in a dark spot between houses, following along like evil shadows, their footsteps echoing in the night like little heartbeats? Or had they suddenly appeared out of nowhere, surrounding her, just wanting to give her a little Halloween scare?

How terrifying it must have been, hearing those footfalls in the darkness. That must've been what impelled her back toward the school. Is that when her hair had begun to come out of its braids? Or was that later, inside the dark pantry? Why hadn't she run toward her own house, or even back to Mom's?

Perhaps she'd simply panicked and rushed headlong back to the place where she thought people were still gathered. She probably had rushed inside, looking for help, but finding none. How long had she waited in that pitch-black pantry before deciding to stack up the chairs and try for that half-open window?

"Why?" I yelled at Mr. Green. "Why did you chase her? Why didn't you and your friends just let her go home?" My voice was quivering I was so upset. Having the bully who was responsible for her death standing right in front of me was almost too much. I kept remembering the day we came upon Sally, standing beside my bed, attempting to pick up Sarey and realizing she never could.

Mr. Green backed up a step. I thought it was because of my anger, but then I felt her, the phantom student. She was hovering somewhere nearby. Gramps put his hand on my shoulder.

"We never meant for her to get hurt," the other man said. And then he turned away, clasping his arms as if for warmth. "I done my time in Juvie. I ain't talking about it no more." He stalked off down the street. "C'mon, Fred," he called without turning around. "We're done here."

He didn't have to tell Fred twice. I think he could see Sally Jean again. He began to run, and he was still running when he turned the corner headed toward home. After a few seconds of Sally shadowing him like the negative image on Gran's land camera film, Mr. Green began to run, too. And then he began to swat at his head just like Fred had done in the cafeteria.

"I'll be making a report to the police," Mrs. Pavey called after him. "Your boy needs to learn a lesson."

If he heard her, he didn't acknowledge it. He simply picked up speed, wind- milling his arms wildly about his head and face. As he turned the corner, we could hear him begin to curse.

If I hadn't been so upset, I might have laughed. But I was still fuming. "Can they just leave like that?" I asked Gramps. "Are they just going to get away with almost getting Derol killed?"

Gramps still had a hand on my shoulder. He could feel me quaking, and I was embarrassed. I'd never been so mad and disgusted in my entire life. Now that I knew how Sally Jean had died, like an animal in a trap, it made me furious.

"We're going down to the PD now. We'll fill out a report and the juvenile officers will go and talk to Fred and his friends. They will probably be put on probation. They may even be sent to Juvenile Hall to finish the school year. It probably all depends on their attitude when the Juvenile Officer interviews them."

"Is that what happened to Mr. Green, all those years ago?"

Gramps nodded. "Yes, but in that case, with a death, he was sent away until he turned eighteen. I don't think he got off easily. I think his conscious will continue to punish him for it from now on."

I took a deep breath and tried to get hold of my emotions. I wasn't so sure Gramps was right this time. If Tank Green's conscious was punishing him, why on Earth had his sons turned out just like him?

Jase, who had been strangely silent, squeezed my other shoulder. I hiccupped. I was not going to cry. Why did I always want to cry when I got angry? I took a deep breath and thought of Buddy. For some reason, that calmed me.

Mrs. Pavey was leading Derol to the car. "We'll go straight to the Police Station," she said. "I can take some of the kids." She glanced at the single-cab pickup.

Gramps hurried over and opened the car door to help Derol inside. "That would be great. I'll bring the rest of them down and we'll contact parents and take statements."

"Thank you," she said. Then she turned back to us. We were all standing in a semi-circle, decompressing. "Thanks to all of you. I don't even know what you were talking about that happened so many years ago, but I know what would have happened tonight, to Derol, if you hadn't intervened."

I ran over to the car and leaned inside the open door. "We'll see you in a minute, Franken-Derol. Don't you worry."

He grinned, and his head jerked to the side. I thought it was amazing that he could still smile at all.

"Wait," Jase called. "Derol's bike." He sprinted over to the tall weeds and stood it up.

"Put it in the bed of the truck," Gramps said. "We'll take it home later."

I went back to pick up his lock and chain, and that's when I glanced down inside the still-open entrance and saw Sally Jean for the very last time. I think she was showing me how her story had ended.

She was lying beneath the wooden stairs, except, in this version, they were not broken. They looked whole and stout, as they must have when she was a student here. Now, only her pale hair was visible in the deep shadows. If it hadn't shone so brilliantly in the faint beam of moonlight falling through the gap, I probably wouldn't have noticed her at all. As I watched, she sat up and peered eerily out from between the steps before creeping from her hiding place and scurrying toward me. For a moment she was spotlighted in the moonbeam. It was the first time I'd ever seen her with her feet on the ground.

Jase was standing beside me now. We instinctively clasped hands as Sally Jean stopped, smiled hesitantly, and then walked on toward the throng of milling kids.

As she passed through the crowd, a few of them shuddered and rubbed at their arms as if to get warm. Laura shivered so fiercely her sequined flapper dress winked and glimmered and tinkled. A cold blast of air whistled through the archway, telling us winter was on its way.

Sally Jean continued walking down the street, only her hair visible as her black dress blended into the night. In moments, she had merged with a group of ghosts and witches on their last round of trick or treating. When a clump of clouds blocked the moon, she disappeared completely.

26

"You kids hop in the truck and we'll head down to the station," Gramps said as he and Jase moved the welded doors back onto the opening. "I'll get Jack Jimson to come back with his tools and figure out a way to close that thing up for good," he said. "I think we've had enough Halloween hijinks for this year."

We were quite a sight when we pulled up at the Police Station with our truck full of bicycles and creatures of the night. Jase and I looked normal compared to most of the crew. Of course the football players weren't too unusual, not for a small West Texas town, that is.

The first thing we saw when we walked inside was Franken-Derol. He was sitting on a long wooden bench, waiting. I was surprised to see Mayor Stone sitting beside him, talking to him. The Mayor's daughter, Candy, the witch who had been dancing with the warlock, was sitting beside them. Other parents were just arriving to pick up their kids and find out what was going on.

Derol's mom was filling out some papers at the counter. Jelly, the nighttime dispatcher, was on the phone. He was calling the Juvenile Officer, Randy Stout.

Everyone in the room could hear every word he said. That's another thing about small towns, nothing is really secret, not forever anyhow.

The water fountain was getting quite a work out. As was the other phone. Kids were still calling their parents to explain why they had left the school without permission. I hoped those parents were as proud of them as I was. To me, the way they had come to our aid—to Derol's aid—meant we had won. It was almost like a rumble in The Outsiders, except this one had been subtler, more psychological. It was as if Fred had forced each student to decide which side they were on—bullies, or the ones being bullied. Too bad we'd already turned in our timeline book report. We might've been able to work it in somehow. Then I thought, nah. Who would ever believe it?

It was very late when we finally got home. At one point, I had fallen asleep on the sofa in the Chief's office with someone's car blanket thrown over me. Gramps wouldn't leave until he'd interviewed every single student who was there. We didn't even have to take Jase home. His mom and dad arrived shortly after he called them.

We didn't get up early the next day, but when we finally did get around, I called Jase and we agreed to meet at Crossroads Music. I wanted to look for a 45 of Janis Joplin's hit, Piece of My Heart.

"Did you know they called her freak in high school?" I asked Jase as we thumbed through the racks of records.

"Yeah, I heard that on the radio." He held up the single. "Let's pay and go to Dal Paso for a Coke."

I smiled. "You read my mind, but first, I want to go to the library like we planned."

"Okay...but we already found out what happened with Sally Jean." He handed me the record and kept digging. "Didn't we?"

I gazed at the cover wondering how Janis would have turned out if she hadn't been teased and taunted in school, just for being original. Would she have just faded into the background? Become a secretary or something, continued singing only in church on Sundays? Would she still be alive, and happy? Or had she been destined to be different, and to suffer because of it? These were the questions I would put to Jase as we drank our Cokes later, but right now, I wanted to find out why Sally had appeared under those stairs in the cellar when she had clearly died on the cold hard floor of the foyer.

We rode slowly to the library, its glass block front shining like a beacon in the afternoon sun. The entrance was decorated for fall with a sheaf of real straw standing in the middle of a pile of pumpkins. I loved the bright orange and gold colors and the faint barnyard odor of the dry straw.

The research librarian smiled indulgently as she led us downstairs and handed us the big, newspaper-sized book that contained all the articles from the Crossroads Gazette the year Sally Jean had died. The librarian no longer questioned me when I came in to do research. I think she got tired of hearing all my explanations. "Just let me know when you're finished," she said. "And I'll come back and put them away."

I nodded and thanked her, and then we got down to business. It wasn't difficult to find the articles once we located the correct dates. Her death had made all the headlines. TRAGIC ENDING, one read. SAD STATEMENT ABOUT OUR YOUTH, read another. We scoured them all, downstairs in the media room at the public library, me seated in a straight-backed chair much like one of those Sally Jean had stacked up in her attempt to escape that night, and Jase leaning over my shoulder, eyes squinted nearly shut against the dust motes that erupted like spores on a spring breeze each time I turned another page.

It was just as Mr. Green had said. Just as Sally had shown us, all except for one thing...after the janitor had discovered the boys and made them leave that night—and locked the door behind them—they had stuck around, hiding in the bushes until he was gone. They knew Sally Jean was still inside, but they didn't even try to tell anyone. They just hung around to see what she would do. It was all a game to them.

They claimed they were not looking when she stacked up the chairs and fell to her death, convulsing on the floor, alone. Tank Green said they saw her body, later, around midnight, when they finally got up the nerve to sneak in through the old cellar, which wasn't welded shut in those days. "It just had a reg'lar old chain and padlock," Tank had said when the Chief of Police had asked him how they'd gotten back inside. "I just used my dad's bolt cutters." His dad was a mechanic. I guess he had lots of tools lying around.

"Wonder if his dad was a bully, too?" I murmured.

"You know what your Gramps says about apples and seeds," Jase replied.

I sighed. "I sure do."

"Turn the page," he said. "Find out what happened when they found her lying there."

"We crossed the floor in disbelief," the article said. "She looked like a ragdoll, but her neck was twisted and one leg was all bent." I had to stop reading for a moment. This was one of the other boys talking at the hearing they held at the courthouse. He was describing Sally Jean's death scene perfectly.

Jase began to read where I'd left off. "We knew she was dead, and we got scared."

"What did you do," the attorney asked.

"We picked her up and took her down in the old cellar. We hid her body under the stairs."

I didn't realize I had my hands over my ears until Jase gently closed the big book. "It goes on to tell how they kept their secret for hours while Sally's mother and father walked the streets, calling out her name."

"Oh..." the word escaped my lips on a moan. "How awful. When did they finally find her?"

Jase shook his head. He wouldn't look at me. There were tears in his eyes, and I suddenly had the idea that he wasn't thinking of Sally Jean anymore. Maybe he was thinking of his mother's dream about the day Rusty got lost in the department store, and how he kept calling out her name, but she couldn't find him.

I stood and wrapped my arms around his middle.

He laid his cheek on top of my head and I could feel moisture seeping into my hair.

"The paper said your mom finally found her," he whispered. "They said she wouldn't let your Gramps quit searching until they had gone over every inch of the school. Including the cellar."

That was my mom, all right, I wanted to say. She always had to fix things, find the solution. I couldn't say anything. That lump was back in my throat. So I just stood there, hanging onto my best friend, thinking of ghosts and bullies and freaks, and kids who were different like Sally and Derol, and Janis Joplin, and even me. I finally began to think of Buddy, and how much fun we'd had riding him that day. It was the only thing I could do to get my mind out of the past and back into the present. Because the past was over, and we had to let it go.

All except for one question that was bothering me. "Why was there a lock on the inside of that pantry door?" I asked Jase.

He smiled and flipped his clean hair off his forehead. "I

wondered that, too. So while you were napping in the Chief's office last night, I did a little research of my own. Jelly Wardlow went to school there, too. He said that in order for the cellar to be used as a tornado shelter, both doors had to be able to lock from the inside. Otherwise, the wind could just suck the doors right open."

"Wow," I was impressed. "I guess that makes sense. Jelly, huh?"

Jase nodded. "He's all right, isn't he?"

I laughed. "He's one of my favorite people, actually. I wish you had done a little more research and found out why they call him Jelly. Gramps claims he doesn't know. I think he just isn't telling."

We walked up the stairs and told the librarian we were finished.

"Did you find the articles you were looking for?" she asked.

We both nodded. In the back of my mind I was thinking about all the things that hadn't been found. Like, Rusty, for example. He was still M.I.A.

Maybe some questions don't have answers, I thought. But how do you live with that? How does one live with an unsolved mystery?

I would have to ask Jase someday, but not today. Today we were going to forget about that dusty book full of ghosts and go get a Coke. Then we were going to go home to my house and put Janis on the stereo. After that, maybe we'd go by and see what Derol and Billy Bob were doing. I wanted to get a look at Derol's trophy for best boy's costume. He was supposed to pick it up today since the dance had gotten interrupted last night. We didn't even know which girl had won for best costume. Someone said it was a seventh grader named Nancy.

Maybe later we could go visit Buddy, go for another little ride. That was always a good thing to do on a Saturday. "I hope that's the end of our ghost adventures," I told Jase as we got back on our bikes outside the library.

"Me, too," he agreed.

But it wasn't. Not by a long shot. And it was all Mr. Lee's fault. He just had to take us fishing that summer. He and his wife were trying to go on with their lives while waiting for news about Rusty. I think they were also trying to make up for lost time with Jase. They didn't know the campsite they were taking us to was haunted. None of us had ever even heard of Crybaby Bridge.

ABOUT THE AUTHOR

Ann Swann is the author of numerous published short stories and novels.
Stevie-girl and the Phantom Student is book two in The Phantom Series.

To learn more about this author

5 Prince Books
http://www.5princebooks.com/annswann.html

Amazon Author page:
http://tinyurl.com/bmrsong
http://www.annswann.blogspot.com

Read on for an excerpt from Book Three, *Stevie-girl and the Phantom of Crybaby Bridge.*

STEVIE-GIRL AND THE PHANTOM OF CRYBABY BRIDGE

The Phantom Series - Book Three

Ann Swann

The year was 1971 and the time was like that hour between twilight and full dark, you know, that time when anything is possible. That's how it was being young, I felt like the whole world was just waiting for me to blossom, to bloom, or to wither and fail. And while I was waiting for something huge to happen ... life kept on rolling along in fits and starts, never slowing, always moving. Just like Stutter Creek, the one that meandered along beneath Crybaby Bridge.

CHAPTER ONE - STEVIE-GIRL AND THE
PHANTOM OF CRYBABY BRIDGE

The woods grew steadily thicker, the trees steadily taller. We went from travelling down a two-lane road through brushy mesquite and stunted live oak— interspersed with mammoth clumps of prickly pear—to chugging down a narrow red-dirt lane lined with huge cottonwoods, pines, and even something that looked and bloomed like dogwood. In places, the trees actually met in a canopy overhead.

We had just crossed over from Texas into the great state of New Mexico. I began to understand why it was called The Land of Enchantment. We didn't have foliage like this in West Texas. I was amazed and a bit intimidated. At home, I could name every plant and flower I could see. But here, just a few hours away, I was in a new world. It made me feel small and uneasy. It made me realize how insulated my little world really was.

"Isn't it great, Stevie-girl?" Jase asked. He was sitting in the back seat with me. His dad was driving and his mom was riding shotgun. It had been a fairly quiet trip so far. I still couldn't believe Jase's mom had invited me to go with them on their annual camping/fishing trip. You could have knocked me over when my Gramps said okay.

"It's beautiful," I replied. "I can't get over how shady it is, even in the middle of the day." I looked at my best friend. Did he know I'd never spent the night away from home before, except with Karla, before she moved off to California?

I was nervous.

It was just after noon when we pulled into the campsite. The clearing was right on the edge of Copper Lake. From where I stood, it was like looking out at the ocean. I couldn't even see the other shore. I wished I'd packed my sketchpad and charcoal pencils. Art had been my third elective this past school year, and I'd found out I was pretty good at sketching things in nature. I hadn't tried any people yet, but next year, I was planning on taking Drawing II. That was figure drawing. I planned to get up my nerve to ask Jase to let me draw him.

"LAKE LEVEL'S WAY UP," Mr. Lee said. "Had a lot of rain this year." He was unloading the trunk of the car as he spoke.

Staring out across the deep, calm water, I was transfixed. With the sun on its downward trend, the surface of the lake appeared as solid as a sheet of beaten metal. I could see where it got the name.

"It's huge. Are we really going to hike around it?" That had been part of the conversation on the trip up, the desire to hike the entire perimeter.

Mr. Lee laughed and handed me the tent poles. "Don't worry, we never get too carried away. We just hike until we find a good spot to swim or picnic or fish, then we stop. Sometimes we don't even start up again." His voice dropped off sharply and he turned half-away. "At least that's what we did when Rusty was with us. He and Jase were always a lot more interested in swimming than in hiking or fishing."

Rusty is their older son. He went missing when his helicopter was shot down in Vietnam last year. I wanted to pat Mr. Lee on the back or give him a hug the way I would do if it were Gramps or Jase who was hurting, but Mr. Lee was different. Sometimes, it seemed as if he was encased in a brittle shell, one that might crack, or break, if we weren't careful with our words.

Mrs. Lee was even more delicate. She seemed to be fragile through and through, like a very thin icicle, the kind you know will shatter when it falls.

I wondered if that was why they had asked me along on the camping trip, to be some sort of buffer. This was their first trip since Rusty was listed as Missing in Action.

Even if that was the reason they invited me, I didn't mind. I spent a lot of time at their house. And Jase spent a lot of time at mine. It was eerie how different our families were.

At their house, it was always so *quiet*. At my house, even though it was just me and Gramps, we always had noise of some kind. If it wasn't the TV or the radio playing, then it was the two of us trying to harmonize on some old hymn. We might not go to church, but we sure liked the old gospel songs.

I thought the other reason they asked me was simply because it would seem as if they'd given up if they didn't go on their annual trip. Whatever the reason, I was thrilled. Not just thrilled that I had been invited, but thrilled that they were actually making an effort to include Jase in their lives again. For far too long, he'd been sort of like a ghost in his own home.

"Think fast!"

I looked up just in time to catch my bedroll from Jase. Mr. and Mrs. Lee were clearing off space for our two tents, a girl's tent and a guy's tent. Mrs. Lee had actually brought a broom—I was pretty sure I'd seen it in their barn—and was sweeping away small sticks and stones while Mr. Lee removed the larger twigs and branches from the area where the tents would be.

"C'mon, Stevie-girl," Jase said. "Let's go gather some fire-stones and firewood. When we get back, we'll finish setting up."

I plopped my sleeping-bag-bedroll on the pile of supplies and followed Jase toward the shore of the lake.

"Not too far," Mr. Lee said. "We'll need those fire supplies before sunset. Besides, you know how quickly darkness falls in the woods . . ."

"Yes sir," Jase replied. "We're just going to check out Crybaby Bridge, Stevie can't wait to hear the baby." He chuckled. It was our little joke.

I laughed, too. But with our history of attracting spirits and phantoms, I wasn't *really* certain I wanted to venture toward Crybaby Bridge. Not just yet, anyhow. Maybe tomorrow, in the early *morning* light.

There was no slowing Jase, though. He just kept strolling along, not even noticing how the tree shadows were growing denser and denser the deeper we went. Silly boy. He was still under the mistaken impression that I was brave.

"I can't believe we'll be in high school in a couple of months." My voice sounded loud in the woodsy silence. I laughed again to cover my nervousness.

"Me either." Jase flipped his long hair off his forehead and swatted a mosquito. They weren't bad right now, in the afternoon, but they would probably get a lot worse in the evening. I wondered why that was. Did they do it because they were storing up food for overnight? Maybe I could research it when I got home. I loved researching things . . .

"I *said*, I can't wait to finish high school and get out of Crossroads." Jase had stopped walking and was waiting on me to catch up both physically and mentally.

"Sorry." I smiled. He was always catching me woolgathering, mulling things over, not paying attention. "But we haven't even got started on high school yet."

"True." His expression was thoughtful. "But after we *do* finish, we get to head off to college, where I can concentrate on writing stories and novels that people will read and talk about and still be reading long after I'm dead." He stopped abruptly, as if considering what he'd just said. "But before that, I might want to go out on the road like Jack Kerouac or Steinbeck and Charley …"

I know he didn't mean to break my heart when he looked so happy contemplating leaving me behind, but I just couldn't quite picture myself in a big college the way he could. My Gramps had those ambitions for me, but the thought of going off to school, to live in a dorm with a bunch of people I didn't know, literally made me nauseous.

I guess Jase didn't notice my hesitation, though. He kept right on talking. "I just want to experience life. How can I write about it if I don't experience it?" His voice sounded stretched, like a rubber band. I thought it might break if I pushed him to explain further.

Jase had recently written a short story about a girl who felt as if she was alone when in reality she was surrounded by people who loved her. Jase had written the story as science fiction—he'd placed the girl on another planet surrounded by invisible beings that wouldn't become visible until she acknowledged them.

I wondered if the story was really about me, but I didn't have the nerve to ask. I was sort of afraid to know. Loneliness was a recurring theme in our lives. Late at night, I often recalled what the phantom pilot said when Jase had first encountered him standing beside his small, upside-down plane. Jase had asked him if anyone else was in the plane.

"I was alone," he'd answered. "We all are." The pilot had uttered those words just as Jase was preparing to stick his head inside the ink-black cockpit of the crashed plane.

Those words had chilled me, and yet, sometimes they comforted me. We're all alone, he'd said. How could that comfort me? I think because it absolved me of any responsibility, any duty, to go out and try to interact with people, to change my personality. I was a loner. I didn't want to worry about other people. I had my Gramps, I had Jase, and on the fringes, I had Billy, Derol, and Karla (well, long distance, that is). The words of the pilot seemed to say that it doesn't matter if you have one friend or one hundred; in the end, we are all alone.

Guess that's why I didn't quite share Jase's wanderlust. He was always more outgoing, more ready to experience new things. When I said that to him once, he'd replied, "But you're the one who went in the haunted house." Then he'd looked at me as if I were crazy. "You're the one who's brave, Stevie-girl. I just follow your lead."

Thinking about it later, I decided that I liked the way he saw me, even if it wasn't quite true.

I don't know what it was about Jase. He wasn't what you'd call an extrovert. He didn't go and seek out other people's attention or approval, but maybe as a result of that, people sought him out. They respected him. He wasn't a jock, he only ran track, he said, because he loved to run, and while he was running he could create scenarios in his head, make up new characters. (Plus, his dad loved sports, so I think he did track mainly so he and his dad would have some place to connect.) Many times, his folks couldn't even make it to the football games where Jase carried a drum in the marching band. I thought it was because Rusty had excelled at football when he was in school.

On lonely nights, I'd sometimes lie in my bed wondering just what it was that drew other kids to Jase. At first I'd thought it was his height, or his good looks, maybe even his kindness toward everyone. But I didn't really think it was any of those completely. Oh, that may be why all the girls responded to him, developed crushes on him, but it didn't explain why even the other jocks—who couldn't care less about looks or kindness—seemed to respect him.

I'd discovered this quality about my best friend when Derol Pavey came to our school and we had to be his voice. That's when I noticed that others literally stopped talking and listened when Jase spoke in class. And that awful night, when we had to hurry to the old abandoned school and rescue Derol from the bullies, almost the entire gym emptied as people left the dance and followed Jase.

I was convinced he had some inner something that others responded to. It will make him a great writer someday, I thought. It will take him far, far away from Crossroads, Texas. Away from me.

ALL AT ONCE, the lane ended and the creek appeared. It was wide, but it didn't look that deep, except maybe right in the middle. The bridge though, it looked ancient, its wide planks gray and warped. It sat atop thick support posts sunk into the streambed. Along the edges, the water slipped and slurped and kicked along over the rocks and foliage lining the banks on each side.

"Guess I know why it's called Stutter Creek," I said, watching the current stop and start and meander along.

"Yeah, it does sort of stutter along, doesn't it?" Jase replied.

We grinned at each other. We both knew we'd be back to explore it more thoroughly after we'd finished setting set up camp.

I guess that's why he thought I was brave. I could never pass up a challenge, no matter how much it frightened me.

"C'mon." He took my hand. "We'd better get some wood and

find some big stones for the fire pit." He glanced at the sky. Under the canopy of the forest, it was very dim.

I squeezed his fingers. I hoped nothing would ever come between us, but just then a chill wind tore across the bridge and flung dirt and leaf debris directly into our faces. We dropped hands and rubbed our eyes in disbelief.

Jase muttered, "What the heck was that?"

I rubbed my vision clear and gazed into the gathering gloom at the opposite end of the bridge. The wind whistled and whirled around our ankles like dusty water.

"I hope that doesn't mean a storm is coming," I said. But that's not what I was really thinking. What I really thought was, *what is it that doesn't want us here?* I couldn't see anything. In fact, the way the crackly leaves were swirling, it was all I could do to see where to place my feet as I stumbled along behind Jase as we made our way back toward the campsite. When I ran my tongue across my teeth, I could feel the grit coating them. I closed my mouth and shielded my eyes.

AFTER A BIT, we realized the wind had died down to a gusty breeze. We looked at each other in silence, then we began to pick up as many dry twigs and branches as we could find. We weren't strangers to strange happenings. But that didn't mean we liked them. Not by a long shot.

WE WALKED ALONG, each of us lost in our own thoughts. It didn't take long to traverse the short distance back. It wasn't far at all, but when we arrived, it was a different world. There was no wind. No flying dust. The camp was just as we'd left it. His parents had finished clearing the area. They had one tent set up and were working on the other.

Jase dropped his armload of braches and ran to help with the confusing jumble of strings, stakes, and poles. I dropped my own batch of sticks and twigs and began to search for large stones for the fire ring. They weren't hard to find, apparently this was a popular place for campers. Either that, or these were the very same stones the Lee family used every year. They were about the size of bowling balls, some larger and squarer, and they were black on one side. They weren't very far from the camp, just slightly scattered.

I gathered all the stones into a circle in what I hoped was the appropriate place. It wasn't too hard to tell where the fires had been laid in previous campouts, not only were there two large logs placed in an L shape in the clearing, but when I swiped away the new carpet of dead leaves and other forest debris, the ground below was still a scorched-earth color, too. Just like the rocks.

"Good job, Stevie-girl," Mr. Lee said.

I didn't realize he was behind me until he spoke. "Thanks," I replied. "I hope this is the right place for the fire . . ."

"Perfect." His voice was kind. "I like the way you don't wait around for someone to tell you what to do. That's the mark of a true camper." He reached over and patted my shoulder curtly. For a moment, I thought he was going to tug the tip of my streaky, brown braid the way Jase always did.

www.ingramcontent.com/pod-product-compliance
Lightning Source LLC
Chambersburg PA
CBHW022005010726
47494CB00003B/903